Bessie's Pillow

A Young Immigrant's Journey
— Based on a true story —

Linda Bress Silbert

Strong Learning Publications
New York

Bessie's Pillow

A Young Immigrant's Journey
by Linda Bress Silbert

Published by Strong Learning, Inc.
Mahopac, NY 10541

www.BessiesPillow.com
www.StrongLearning.com

ISBN: 978-0-89544-201-7

Printed in the United States of America.

10 9 8 7 6 5 4 3 2 1

Unless otherwise noted, all photographs used in *Bessie's Pillow*
were provided by the author. Because no photographs of Boshka Markman as
a young woman are known to be in existence, the image of the young girl on
the cover is derived from an early photograph of the author's mother, Bessie
Dreizen's daughter Ann.

The image of the *S.S. Moltke* on the cover is a derivative of a photograph from
the collections of the Gjenvick-Gjønvik Archives and is used with permission.

Lovingly dedicated to the memory of
Ann Dreizen Bress
1915-2012

The New Colossus

Not like the brazen giant of Greek fame
With conquering limbs astride from land to land;
Here at our sea-washed, sunset gates shall stand
A mighty woman with a torch, whose flame
Is the imprisoned lightning, and her name
Mother of Exiles. From her beacon-hand
Glows world-wide welcome; her mild eyes command
The air-bridged harbor that twin cities frame,
"Keep, ancient lands, your storied pomp!" cries she
With silent lips. "Give me your tired, your poor,
Your huddled masses yearning to breathe free,
The wretched refuse of your teeming shore,
Send these, the homeless, tempest-tossed to me,
I lift my lamp beside the golden door!"

— Emma Lazarus —
New York City, 1883
in anticipation of the installment of the
Statue of Liberty

Prologue

New Rochelle, 1950

❖

It wasn't my time to die back in 1906. The mobs, the murder, the rape. The blood running through the streets of the Pale. I escaped because it wasn't my time. Instead I lived—a young woman of eighteen years, I traveled to America and escaped the Pale.

This isn't the story of my escape. This is the story of my arrival and the journey of building a new life in a strange land. It's the story of one life's grief and happiness. Of struggle and success. Of the desperation and hope that drove me and countless immigrants to leave our homes and families behind and build again.

No matter what put us on that boat or what happened along the way, when we came to America, we did our best. For ourselves, for our children and for their children.

We would all have challenges, some greater than others. Sometimes indescribable happiness prevailed for me and at other times, I was forced to hide both my fear and my pain. Unlike so many, I was fortunate to have the opportunities I did and the people who were in my life. For that I am grateful. Especially for the people.

Of one sort or another, no matter who you are, you will face many challenges. It is no different today. It will be no different tomorrow. But, whatever those challenges, know that I am with you, as are countless others long gone.

All will be well. Happiness will come again.

Part One
Leaving Home

1

Vilna, Lithuania
1906

⊹⇒◎⇐⊹

I can't find Tateh or Mamaleh. I lost them in the crowd—we were separated while I was saying goodbye to our neighbors. All of us made the long trip to Vilna in my father's wagon.

It is early January and my breath condenses in the cold air. As I pull my coat closer around me, I am aware of people speaking in Russian, Lithuanian, even Polish. I hear Yiddish too, but in Glubokoye, where I grew up, we speak it only to each other and behind closed doors. Children run by me, brushing against my legs, while adults huddle and pray, holding onto each other knowing they will never see each other again. We are one of those families—Mamaleh, Tateh, my brothers and me. Just 18 years old, I am leaving today for America…alone.

Lithuania, once independent, is now part of the Russian Empire and within the Pale of Settlement, an area in which Jewish people are forced to live together like cattle.

I hear a loud whistle, a warning that the train will leave soon, and I am frightened because I still don't see my family. I am not even five feet tall and it is hard for me to see over the heads in the crowd.

I push against people who reek of labor and servitude. Though the odor is awful, I understand—they have few clothes and are too poor to bathe often.

I, on the other hand, will be tidy throughout my journey from Glubokoye to Hamburg and then to America. My new skirt is made of gray wool, perfect for traveling. My shirtwaist is a lighter gray cotton broadcloth with pretty tucks on the bodice, a high collar, and sleeves buttoned at the wrist. A long dark blue cloak with a hood keeps the bitter wind from my face. I drew the patterns for my wardrobe myself. The dressmaker in Glubokoye who made my clothing told me I'd done a good job. I have decided that I will be a dressmaker in America.

Tears burn my eyes in the cold air. Panicking, I begin to run. Nothing I see is familiar. Before today, I only traveled to Vilna once— Tateh brought me with him on one of his trips to buy goods to sell. I'm sure Mamaleh disapproved of my going, but in Jewish households husbands make decisions about important things like who will travel. I don't think it is right for husbands to do all of the deciding. That time, however, because Tateh decided that I should go with him, I was very glad indeed.

I see Tateh ahead and continue to run even faster. I fall on a patch of ice and look up to see his gloved hand reaching out to me. My heart leaps—I love my father very much. I take his hand and he pulls me up. Our eyes meet and it is then that we both realize this may be the last time he will be there when I fall.

—◉—

It is late in the day and I am riding in the wagon with my father to make his deliveries. "Tateh," I ask, "why did you stop being a rabbi and start selling pots and buckets?"

My father smiles at my inquisitiveness. "Because I like to sell pots and buckets."

We ride for a long time in silence before Tateh speaks again. "Sometimes one cannot do everything one wants, Boshka. It is better for Mamaleh and your brothers and you for me to sell things than for me to be a rabbi. I sell things to keep you safe. Someday you'll understand."

I don't say anything, but though I am only twelve, I already understand. Too much. I know about the rabbi who was dragged from his house by the Czar's men and never seen again. I know about the pogroms. I know about the men conscripted and never heard from again.

"I can't imagine not being able to do things I want to do," I say.

Tateh smiles, but his eyes are sad. "I know, Boshka. I know."

—◉—

After I brush myself off, I see Mamaleh off to the side, balancing my youngest brother on her hip while she holds the hand of another. Max and Jack, the two oldest of my four brothers, lean against a storefront apart from the chaos. As I walk toward them, I can see my mother is crying. She looks away, but when I reach her, I turn her face toward me with my hands.

"It's fine, Mamaleh," I say. "I'll be happy in America. And safe."

"Yes," she says.

A gust of wind chills all of us and we shiver. Tateh points to the train. "There's not much time left." In response, my mother wipes her eyes and recites a litany of directives.

"Stay away from treif. You must eat what our people eat. The others may eat treif, but not you."

"Yes, Mamaleh."

"And beware of passengers on the train or boat with odd-looking eyes. They could have trachoma—they can send you back if you have trachoma."

"Yes, Mamaleh."

"Stay away from anyone or anything that looks suspicious. Use the good mind that God has given you."

I nod.

"Let's go over the plan one more time. Do you have the paper with the addresses?"

"Yes, Mamaleh," I say, patting the pocket of my coat. "When I get to New York, I will go directly to Lillian's house at a place called the Upper West Side. I will live with her and her husband, but if I am not happy there, I will go to our friends Miriam and Lou Schaffer. They live in a part of the city called Washington Heights."

I think of Lillian and Miriam. Lillian is my half-sister—she is Tateh's daughter too. After her mother, Tateh's first wife, died he sent her to New York to live with his sisters. Now that she is grown, he receives letters from her. She is doing very well in America—she married a German Jew named Lazar Bechhofer. He is very rich.

Miriam was my best friend in Glubokoye when we were children. Miriam and I were inseparable. We played together by the lake in the summertime and ran through the hills, giggling and jumping into the water when the boys weren't around. Lou is her older brother. She is now an American, living well-off like Lillian—with Lou, whom she says has made a lot of money selling coffee and tea. It seems anyone can be successful in America.

My father's voice interrupts my reverie. "Tell your brothers good-bye now, Boshka."

I nod and give each of them a hug. "Max...Jack...," I say, while holding both their hands, "I will send for you once I'm settled. I'll find a way to get you to America. You won't have to go into the army. I promise." They smile at me and nod, though I can tell they do not believe me.

I reach out to hug Tateh when someone taps my shoulder. It is a woman not much taller than I. "Excuse me. I hope you remember me from Glubokoye—I am Chana Dreizen. I couldn't help overhearing that you are traveling to New York. My son is there and I need to get something to him. I thought my cousin would be here, but I haven't seen her. I am hoping you will take it to him instead." She removes from a burlap sack a feather pillow embroidered with flowers. "I made it for him to take to America but he left it behind. He has written to me about it now several times."

Tateh responds to her. "Of course, we remember you, Mrs. Dreizen. Max and Jack used to play with your sons." He nods a silent approval for me to take the pillow.

The woman turns back to me. "Please find him and give it to him. I will write to him that you are coming."

I look down at the pillow—in the midst of the flowers, there is a Yiddish phrase: *May this pillow bring you peace.* I open one of my bags and push the pillow into it. "How will I find him?"

"His name is Nathan. Nathan Dreizen." She says his name again. "There is an aid society for immigrants in New York. The members of the Glubokoye Society will help you to find him. He lives in a town called New Rochelle."

I am thinking that Lillian will know about the society. I repeat the name to myself two times, but decide I will probably forget it. I take out the piece of paper with Lillian and Miriam's addresses and write it down on the back.

Nathan Dreizen
New Rochelle

The whistle blows, this time much louder, and a conductor yells that the train will be leaving in less than ten minutes. Mrs. Dreizen thanks me again and kisses me on the cheek. Before she disappears into the crowd she adds, "Darling, it's a long trip. You are welcome to use the pillow if you like."

Tateh takes one of my hands and Mamaleh takes the other. I cannot suppress the thought that they will not dance at my wedding and that Mamaleh will never hold my children on her lap. Tears stream down my face and soon we are sobbing like all the other families around us. The whistle sounds again and Tateh pats me on the back. "You must go now, Boshka."

A man picks up my bags and valise, and I hurry behind him to the front of the train where the first-class cars are located. When I climb the steps to board the train, I look back, but I can no longer find them in the crowd.

2

❖⟫●⟨❖

When I am settled into my seat, I look out the window at a sea of sad faces and waving hands. I wonder for a moment if what I have will be enough in America, but then feel ashamed. I am carrying two lovely new carpetbags and a small valise. Many clutch sacks of food and small burlap bundles that hold all their worldly possessions.

In Glubokoye, mine was a better life than for some because Tateh has money. He sells hardware to the Russians and in exchange, they allow him to keep some of his money, though they tax him heavily and demand bribes. The government refers to Tateh as a "useful" Jew, and because of that, our family has not suffered the fate of many of the other families who live in poverty in the Pale.

Once it pulls away from Vilna, the train rolls along past fields of snow. Gray clouds whisk by and I lay my head against the window. An image of the pillow comes to me and I take it out of my bag. Sinking my head into its soft feathers, I close my eyes but I'm too excited and anxious to sleep, so I sit up and pull out the Yiddish newspaper Tateh picked up for me at the train station.

In addition to Yiddish, I speak Lithuanian, Russian and German, and can read and understand Polish if it is spoken slowly. At home, I always spoke Yiddish with my family, but Miriam wrote me that this will change if I am to succeed in America.

It's been less than an hour and already I miss Glubokoye, my family, my friends, Tateh's customers whom I've come to know. As I look out the window, I can see hills and a lake that reminds me of Lake Berezvetshe. I think about Kopanitze, the loveliest area in the park where, when I was younger, I played with Miriam and neighborhood friends on Shabbos afternoons. Tears spring to my eyes and I quickly realize that I must force these pictures from my mind or I will be tempted to turn back.

To compose myself, I remember all that is not good in the Pale. After the uprising last year, the Russians conceded many rights to Lithuanians, but not to all of us. My parents thought surely we Jews would not be far behind, but I doubted it. A few months before, a teenaged Litviner boy had taunted me, rushing out to the road to throw stones at me as I walked home from school. His words were telling—he heard them at home or at school as he could not have thought of them by himself.

Jewish families in the Pale live in constant fear of the pogroms— the angry mobs of the Russian police, peasants, even men in military uniforms who storm drunk through the streets. The Czar encourages the torture, rape and killing of Jews. Forcing us to live in one place makes that easier for them.

Once, while peeking through the cracks in our shutters, I saw a man in a uniform break down the door of my neighbor's house, drag Mamaleh's friend into the yard and begin to beat her with his fists. I looked away and put my hands over my ears, but not soon enough to avoid hearing her screams.

As Mamaleh often entreated me, I hid in my house when the mobs came to our town. If a group of them ever came near while I was alone in the house, I was to call out, as loudly as possible, the names of all the Jewish men I knew.

I force my mind back to the present. What will Lillian look like? Will she wear diamonds and gold, velvet gowns trimmed with lace? I'm nervous to meet her, but she is my sister and I'm sure she will welcome me. Lazar, her husband, has agreed that I can live with them so Tateh says he must be a fine person. I look forward to meeting him.

I am eager, also, to see one of the picture shows Miriam has written and raved about, like "The Great Train Robbery" and "A Gentleman of France." And I want to eat in American restaurants. I hope they are kosher—Tateh and Mamaleh will be disappointed in me if I eat treif.

After another hour or so, the train finally makes its first stop and I step out of the train for some fresh air. The journey to Hamburg will last three days and already I am weary. I remind myself that when I get there, I'll be one step closer to America.

3

Hamburg, Germany

I have arrived in Hamburg, where I will wait to be washed, disinfected and inspected by doctors and other officials before we embark. I'm told they are very careful because the shipping line will have to bear the expense if I am returned for any reason.

I'll be staying in a lodging house near the barracks that has ties to the passenger ships. I've heard that the lodging house has no single rooms so I'll have to share a room with strangers. I was hoping to go through the inspection process privately, but I am told even the first-class passengers are required to report to the barracks in two days.

I go back and forth between happiness anticipating my new life and sadness for leaving my old one. I am most sad when I see passengers traveling as families—mothers holding babies and minding their little ones while fathers, speaking Yiddish, smoke together and discuss politics in "the old country." They may have been away from their home for three days but their home travels *with* them as long as they're together.

A woman in the dining car tells me that we are to be washed and processed like everyone else. Because it will be close quarters, I could easily catch a disease from another woman. Another passenger on the train told me that first-class passengers go through the process in a separate room from third-class, which makes me feel less anxious, but only for a little while. At the next stop, an older man with a hacking cough climbs on. Everyone looked so nervous that the man ended up sitting by himself. It is obvious that whether first-class or third, a person can be rejected for the smallest flaw.

Finally, the train reaches Hamburg and we disembark. As I walk in search of the lodging house, I look around at the city. Stone buildings with peaked roofs stand tall and canals snake through the city. The streets bustle with people speaking many different languages but I hear mostly German. I'm surprised at the damp and windy coldness of Hamburg so different from the cold in Glubokoye. I realize that I've never been this close to the sea.

Other first-class passengers are in the lodging house with me, and I've had dinner with a few German ladies who will join their husbands who are businessmen in America. We all sit at one big table where kosher food is served on heavy platters. Large bowls are passed from one person to the next.

Speaking a crisp German Yiddish, they treat me like a child because I am small and much younger than they. They talk as if they're superior to me, as if I should feel fortunate that they've accepted me into their circle. They speak of selling goods as being a low occupation and laugh at the idea of a "useful" Jew. Instead of telling them about Tateh, I concentrate on cutting up my meat and potatoes. By the second dinner, I am offended that for two nights in a row they've discussed how disgusting the Russian Jews are right in front of me.

"*I'm* from Lithuania. *I'm* a Russian Jew," I say.

"Child," they respond, "you aren't at all like the filthy livestock crammed into the barracks. You are a little lady, and we will see to it that you remain so."

The ladies say that their husbands have purchased houses called "brownstones" in the wealthy German-Jewish section of New York City but that the Russian Jews live in poverty just as they do in the Pale—in Glubokoye and Vilna. When I hear this, I nearly choke. I thought everyone had an opportunity in America, even the poor—I wonder how it is that Lillian and Lazar are rich.

I excuse myself from dinner, complaining of a headache. As I walk away from the table, I hear one of them say, "Poor thing, she misses her family terribly." I do miss my family, but it is *they* who gave me the headache!

Since that first day on the train, I have been glad Mrs. Dreizen asked me to deliver the pillow. I curl into a ball and hold it against me until I fall asleep. During the daytime, I can distract myself by walking around Hamburg or listening to the gossip of the ladies at meals. But at night, I am lonely—having the pillow comforts me.

On the third morning in Hamburg, I am startled when the German ladies knock on my door, saying it is time for us to go through a disinfection and inspection process. On the way to the barracks, they are not so talkative.

We stand in line for more than an hour with other first-class passengers and then are herded into a huge room. I hear wailing. When I ask one of the women what is happening, she tells me that a third-class passenger has been turned away. The one named Rivka leans over and whispers into my ear. "Just listen to what animals they are!"

I don't respond—I'm happy to be traveling in first class, but I can't help feeling sorry for those in steerage. It's obvious that some of the noise is nothing more than children playing and babies crying, but there's no point in telling Rivka how I feel.

When it's my turn, the processor takes my papers and examines them. "Go to room one, the ladies' chamber," he says in German as he hands me back my documents. I go up the stairs, following the crowd of women, and we wait in the hall for hours.

Boredom and hunger have replaced my nervousness by the time the inspector finally beckons to my group, directing us down another hall to a large room with a tile floor and benches along the walls. "You will undress so the women inspectors can bathe you," he says. The door slams behind him and we all look at each other.

I've never undressed in front of strangers before and I doubt the other ladies have either. We look around at each other until an older woman begins to unbutton her shirtwaist, and the rest of us do the same. Soon we're all standing with eyes downcast, trying to cover our nakedness with our arms.

I shiver and hug myself to keep warm as we wait for yet another hour. Finally, the inspectors—all of whom are large German women with square jaws—enter the room. They instruct us to stand in a straight line. The German Jews and those Russian Jews like me, who understand German, move without hesitation. The others follow our example.

The inspectors proceed to scrub every part of our bodies with harsh soap and cold water. I continue to stare straight ahead but shiver and blush as the woman cleans my private areas. She notices my reaction. "You must be cleaned thoroughly," she says. To her, it is merely a job—it is as if I am a lamp to be dusted or a spoon to be washed.

The German women work with diligence, spending equal time on each woman and then moving quickly to the next. When the scrubbing ends, the inspectors turn on the showers and we take turns rinsing ourselves. Once we finish, we stand dripping wet and cold until the inspectors give us each two rough towels.

A woman in charge barks commands. "Use one towel to dry yourself off. Put that towel in this container when you are finished. Use the other towel to wrap yourself in so you stay warm. We will take your clothes and wash them thoroughly and disinfect them. They will be ready by day's end." I sigh. I am not looking forward to more waiting.

In yet another large room, hundreds of us sit wrapped in towels on wooden benches like those in a train station. Rivka, Rebecca and Judith sit close to me gossiping about how fat or unattractive some of the women are.

"These women are nothing but yentas," I think to myself, and then close my eyes and wish Mamaleh were here with me. She would smile and kiss me on the forehead and remind me to be patient.

Next, doctors come down the line to inspect each of us. Shaking again, I stand up for my turn. The doctor smiles at me as he examines my face, looks inside my nose, mouth and ears. He taps and feels all over my body. "She's healthy," he says to the woman behind him with the pen and paper, and I finally relax. Once the examinations are finished, we receive water and a bowl of cold soup with potatoes in it. By now, I'm thankful for anything to eat.

At the end of the day, the inspectors return our clothes, which now smell of disinfectant. We are told to report to the barracks in the morning, this time with all our possessions so they can be disinfected and inspected also.

I pass this inspection as well and return to wandering about Hamburg, looking into shop windows and watching the crowds of people. I eat dinner with the yentas each evening before retiring to sleep with the pillow snuggled close. And then early one morning, a foghorn awakes me, and I am happy—it is the big steamship that will take me to America.

4

⊶⊷

I nearly cry when I discover we must go through another inspection and medical examination, but on the day of embarkation, everyone arrives early. I want to feel confident and look my best when I walk onto the ship. I put on my blue velvet dress and brush my hair one hundred strokes so it will be shiny. Yesterday, I paid a young man to polish my boots.

A carriage takes the yentas and me to the passenger hall with all of our possessions. They carry fewer bags than I—most of their clothes, hats, shoes, fine china, family photographs and more have been packed in large trunks to be stored on the ship. They do not know that I am carrying all that I own.

As we drive through the streets, I watch the people walking about again and a voice in my head speaks. "Stay in Hamburg," it says. I scold myself.

Everyone pushes their way to the front of the lines for yet more waiting. Thank goodness, this time only our possessions are inspected.

An official puts stickers that read "Inspected" on each carpet bag and my valise. A doctor briefly examines me and gives me a vaccination. He then puts a sticker on my passenger ticket that reads "Medically Examined," pats my head, and moves on to the next woman in line.

Another official hands me a vaccination card and stamps my ticket. "United States Consulate-General, Hamburg," it says. It's official—I'm going to America!

My heart is sad for the immigrants who cry out when they don't pass the medical examination. They look tired and hopeless as the police escort them out of the passenger hall. Most will be sent back home to the Pale.

As we walk back through the passenger hall, the police stop us one last time. They are looking for youths attempting to escape conscription, fugitives, and women who may have been kidnapped.

Outside, dinghies wait to carry us to the ship. Rebecca looks at the small boat beside us and frowns. "We have to get into this?"

"Just step down into it," Judith answers, teeth clenched. Even she has grown tired of her friend's behavior.

I ignore their bickering and step into the dinghy, concentrating on keeping my balance as the boat bobs up and down. Once seated on the wooden bench with my bags tucked securely underneath, I look out to sea. The *S.S. Moltke*, one of the magnificent steamships of the Hamburg-American Line, awaits us.

The bottom of the ship is painted black and has hundreds of windows. Two large black stacks blow gray smoke. I see an American flag waving from one of the masts. I get tears in my eyes again, but this time they're tears of joy.

Soon the dinghy is next to the ship and the yentas step cautiously onto the gangplank. I follow closely behind. Once aboard, yet another line forms and I wait impatiently, wondering once again if the lines will ever end.

Finally, it's my turn. A man holds out his hand and speaks to me. "Documents, little miss," he says in German. I give them to him, and he scans the manifest until he finds my name.

"Boshka Markman," he says, "you are in first class. Take these stairs two flights up where you will find a steward. He'll show you to your stateroom."

"*Danke*," I say as I take back my documents. Before I start up the stairs, I take one last look behind me and say goodbye to my homeland.

I climb the stairs and after looking at my papers, the steward leads me to my stateroom. I am somewhat embarrassed to be traveling first class but because I am a young woman alone, Tateh refused to allow me to travel in second class or in steerage with the poorest people. He'd heard that even in second class, people share rooms and sometimes other passengers steal things—even documents.

My room, which is painted a soft white, looks elegant in contrast to a dark wood dresser and carpeted floor. One half of the dresser has drawers for clothing and undergarments, and the other half has a sink and faucet. Built into the dresser at the very top is a mirror. I'm glad for the mirror, but it is so high, I won't be able to use it without standing on a chair.

A bed extends from one wall to another with a railing that can be raised to keep me from falling out if the seas are rough. Curtains hang in front of the bed for warmth. Completing the room are a settee with floral upholstery and a white rattan chair.

There are three windows with wooden blinds and velvet curtains. I think I will be able to sleep well at night listening to the sounds of the sea.

The steward speaks to me in German. He looks at the two carpet bags and valise. "Miss, do you have other baggage?"

"Nein. Only these."

"Very well." He hands me a piece of paper. "At your leisure, please familiarize yourself with the first-class information and rules. The rules are also on the announcement board outside the dining hall."

"*Danke.*"

"If you need anything, the other stewards and I are happy to attend to anything you want at any time. Enjoy your passage, and please remember dinner is in an hour at 6:30 p.m."

He shuts the door behind him and I sit down on the settee. A wave of sadness washes over me—once again, I feel very alone. "Why can't I be strong all the time?" I think to myself as I sniffle and wipe my eyes.

To distract myself, I pick up the first-class rules that the steward gave me and read:

FIRST CLASS CABIN NOTICE

Dining

Breakfast at 8:00 a.m.
Lunch at 12:30 p.m.
Dinner at 6:30 p.m.

A menu is printed for each meal. Seats at tables are assigned by the Chief Steward. A bell will be sounded 15 minutes before each meal, and a second signal at the beginning of the meal. Children paying half fare must dine at the children's table.

Staterooms

The staterooms have electricity. There are connections for an electric curling iron and an electric food warmer. Coffee, tea and milk can be warmed at night with the food warmer.

When the steamer is in port, please lock your staterooms.

Bathing

There are numerous bathrooms aboard.

After a few seconds, I stop reading. I'll figure it out as I go. I'm too tired to read rules. I lie down on my bed and drift asleep, only to be wakened by the sound of a loud bell. I sit up, heart racing.

When I remember where I am and that it is only time for dinner, I lie back for a moment to calm myself and then step off the bed. I carry the rattan chair to the dresser and grab a brush from my valise. I hope I'm at a table with young people I can talk to and not with old ladies who will complain about the food and other passengers.

I step down from the chair, take a small purse from my bag and leave my stateroom. Halfway to the dining room, I decide that I'll take a walk on the deck after dinner and run back to get my cloak.

As I begin to make my way to the dining room again, I realize the *Moltke* has sailed. With all the commotion, I'd forgotten to watch the ship move out from the harbor.

I walk down the wooden hallway until I reach a grand hallway and a spiral staircase. A sign says "Smoking Room" with an arrow pointing downstairs. I continue to walk until I reach the first-class dining room. There's yet another line but it takes only a minute before I am at the front.

"Your name, miss?" says the man at the entrance.

"Boshka Markman."

He glances at a paper before him. "Table eight. The steward will show you the way."

I enter the dining room and am surprised at how large it is. Red velvet chairs line up perfectly with place settings at tables that must seat fifty people. Most people are already seated, laughing and talking.

The steward and I arrive at table eight and he pulls out the chair for me. At the other end, I see older couples and some single passengers as I wait for others to fill up the seats around me. I take a sip of water, hoping it will keep my stomach from rumbling. A few Germans come, filling all but the last few open seats, and I take another sip of water.

The last of my table finally arrives—two women and a handsome young Jewish man, who immediately catches my eye. He sits down next to me and smiles.

"Hello," he says. "I'm David."

5

David speaks in German.

Flustered, I reply in Yiddish. "I'm Boshka. It is nice to meet you."

He laughs and replies in Yiddish. "Where are you from?"

"Russia. I lived in a town called Glubokoye in Lithuania."

He nods. "I know it. I lived in Courland, outside the Pale of Settlement, north of where you lived. Most Jews in Courland speak German. My grandfather escaped from the Pale and moved to Courland..." His voice trails off when he realizes he is rambling. "Do you speak English?"

"No. I know a few words, but that's all."

"Neither do I. Maybe we can study together?"

"Yes, that would be helpful." I smile but I am nervous. Tateh would be concerned about my acceptance of the offer of a stranger. I decide I shouldn't act so willing to study with him. "But I won't study in the evening. Only during the mornings and after lunch."

I look at the menu and order sliced salmon without the sauce. David orders filet of beef. I ask him if the beef is kosher. "Don't worry," he says. "It's a matter of survival on this boat. We can't only eat fish. And you'll soon get tired of herring. At the breakfast buffet, there are three different kinds, but only herring. No other fish. At lunch sometimes there will be sardines on toast."

I make a face and he tries to reassure me. "The trip is long. God will understand. Look around you. Most of the other Jews are ordering the beef."

I do as he suggests and discover he's right—all around me people are speaking Yiddish and devouring beef. I consider it for a moment, but decide to stay with my original choice.

The other people assigned to our table talk and laugh and drink lots of wine and beer. I don't drink such beverages and I'm pleased to see David doesn't either.

As we continue eating, David tells me more about himself. He's a year older than I am, learned Yiddish from his grandfather, and his family owns a tannery in Liepaja, the capital of Courland. David is traveling to Chicago, a city far from New York, where he will help his older brother Joseph run his business.

"Joseph is my Tateh's name. He is a merchant too. What type of business is your brother Joseph in?"

David smiled. "He started a bank. It's quite successful now. He is going to train me to be the manager."

"That's a good opportunity."

"It is. In his letters, he speaks highly of America. He's traveled to New York and even San Francisco. I'm excited to be there with him, but I will miss Courland…"

David looks down at his empty plate, and I offer him another piece of bread. I want to console him, but it's too forward, so I say, "I feel the same way. I wish my family were here with me."

"I didn't realize it would be so hard."

I nod. "Perhaps we can keep each other company until we get to America."

He offers a weak smile in response. "That makes me feel better."

Waiters remove our plates and glasses, handing us dessert menus as they make their way down the long table. I choose an ice. David watches others ordering fruit tarts and creamy puddings, even cake. Then he looks at me and orders an ice also. When we finish, David asks if I want to walk the deck before heading to my stateroom. "It's cold but we should be able to see the ocean by moonlight."

I'm tempted, but taking a walk with a young man I don't know, even if he is a Jew, would offend Tateh. "No, thank you. I can see the ocean from the windows in my stateroom."

He laughs. "I understand. My mother would scold me for being forward with a pretty young woman I've just met. I'll see you tomorrow at breakfast. Perhaps we can study afterward."

Back in my stateroom, I lie in my bed holding Nathan Dreizen's pillow. The moon is bright and I can see the ocean far into the distance. I decide not to close the curtains and blinds so I will wake with the sun and in a matter of minutes, the sea rocks me to sleep.

After breakfast the next morning, David and I walk out to the promenade deck. The sky is dull and hazy today. My cloak proves useless against the sea wind and frigid air. Today the waves churn as if they're angry at something and I have to hold onto the railing for balance. We walk quickly back inside.

"We should be studying," I say.

"Oh, but it's more fun to explore first. We can study after lunch—we have days."

The cabin decks are at the top of the ship. Below them is the massive kitchen and below that is the steerage class. I hear that the third class passengers are crammed into it and the conditions are harsh. Outside, when I look down to one of the lower decks, I see many of them roaming around, but I can't see much else.

"Can you imagine what it is like in steerage?" I ask David as we turn down another hall toward the library. The ship pitches and I stumble and reach for his arm to steady myself.

"I don't want to. I saw enough in Hamburg. I'm just grateful it's not us."

We find the door to the gymnasium and the grill room, a small restaurant that's always open in case one is hungry between meals. In the ladies' parlor, women sit at tables sipping tea, playing cards or sewing and talking. I see the yentas. They wave and I wave back. Their smiles broaden as they see me with David and I know this will give them a topic for their gossip. In the smoking room, men are talking and laughing. As we walk by, the door opens and someone leaves—the smell of brandy, cigars and cigarettes wafts out.

We see another flight of stairs, but are stopped by a steward who asks where we are going. When David explains, the steward shakes his head. "First-class passengers are not allowed below this level."

Later, after we've seen almost everything on the first- and second-class decks, we decide it is time to study. Another steward directs us to a small library and we spend the morning poring over a German-to-English translation and laughing over what we are sure is our horrible pronunciation. Some of the words are similar, but most are different.

After lunch, I venture to the ladies' parlor and find the yentas there again. They are full of questions. "Who is the handsome young man? Is he rich? Why is he going to America? Is he already established?"

Between sips of tea, I answer their questions as vaguely as I can. Mamaleh taught me to be nice to everyone so I work hard to be pleasant and stay with them for a while.

A woman walks by me and I exclaim. "Her fingernails are bleeding! We cannot go near her. We don't want to catch it! Surely, if we get off the ship with blood in our fingernails the doctor will send us back."

Rivka turns and looks around the room. "Who are you talking about?" I point at the woman but try not to let her know I am talking about her.

"That's not a disease, my dear child," says Judith, giggling at my naïvete. "That's the new rage in Paris. Fashionable women massage red powder or cream into their nails and then rub them until they're shiny."

I am so relieved I don't care that the yentas laugh.

David and I pass the next few days studying, walking on the decks, and eating. Our studying hasn't been very productive—we have learned only a few English phrases. I can now ask for directions and more bread in the dining room.

After dinner each night, I return to my stateroom. After the first night, I allow David to walk with me. After a few days, he moves closer to me when we talk and lingers when we say goodnight.

One afternoon it rains hard. "I remember the rain in Liepaja. It would rain for days on end," David says.

"It was the same in Glubokoye."

"I loved when it rained during holy days. At least when it rained, you knew..." His voice trails off. I know what he's about to say.

"Yes, the rain keeps away the pogroms..." My voice fades too before I can say what I'm thinking.

David stares off into space. "You know why I am really going to Chicago, don't you?"

I think so. Courland is not so far away from the Pale and David is still a Jew.

We are quiet for a moment and then David speaks again. "Have your brothers been conscripted?"

"Not yet. So far, Tateh has been able to bribe the military officials. I don't know how much longer he can keep it up. The amounts they demand are increasing."

The Russians treat Jewish conscripts horribly, even those from outside the Pale, giving them discarded uniforms and worn out boots. During war, Jews are often sent to the front as buffers, often without weapons or ammunition. When they are conscripted, parents in Russia know their sons will die. Several young men we knew well in Glubokoye were conscripted during the Russo-Japanese war. The war ended a few months ago, but none of them returned.

David's voice quiets to a whisper. "Have your brothers...have they hurt themselves?"

Some Jewish boys who are facing conscription will maim themselves to avoid the brutal treatment but are often conscripted anyway.

"One of my neighbors did it," David whispers. "He went to the town doctor and asked him to cut off two toes and the doctor did it."

I shuddered. "Was he refused service?"

"Yes, thank God, yes."

The steamer's captain announces at breakfast that we're now one day away from New York. I thought the voyage might take a full two weeks because of winter weather, but it will only be ten days and I am excited. Everyone hugs and rejoices, including David and me.

"We have to celebrate," David says. "I'll take you for dinner in the grill room later this evening. It won't be crowded like the dining room. We can have our own table."

"That would be nice, David, but it's too much money."

David persists. "I'll be a banker soon. I have plenty of money waiting for me in Chicago."

"All right, then. Thank you."

At eight, I meet David outside the grill room. He's wearing a new suit which makes him look older and more sophisticated. I'm wearing my usual blue velvet dress that he has seen plenty of times.

As we enter the grill room, he extends his arm to me, something he hasn't done before. So grown up, we sit at a table for two in soft romantic lighting. A steward hands us menus.

Throughout dinner, we talk about the weather, the people on the boat, the phrases we've learned in English. David drums his fingers on the table. He seems nervous. That makes me nervous too, even though I'm not sure why.

When it is time to order dessert, David orders French sponge cake with chocolate crème for both of us. I think that it's odd that he ordered for both of us but I don't say anything. It does sound delicious and this is a celebration. I don't complain.

After dessert, I glance at the clock. "It's late and I must get back to my stateroom."

David leans in. "Boshka, I'd like to ask you something."

For some reason, I feel queasy.

"Will you marry me?"

I'm speechless. Seconds pass and words still don't come.

He reaches for my now shaking hand. "I had planned to find a wife in Chicago, but God intervened and I found you. We would make a good life together. I'll be a banker so you can have fine things, and we'd have children. It would be perfect."

I remove my hand from his and take a deep breath. "David, you've been the greatest part of this voyage. When I've felt scared and home-sick, you've made the trip fun and less lonely, and I appreciate that. But you know I can't marry you." I am so uncomfortable that I don't remember anything else I say.

Back in my stateroom I get ready for bed, but tonight I can't sleep. It's too perfect. David is perfect, the time is perfect and yet it doesn't feel right. I toss and turn and then I realize what's wrong.

His American dream is different from mine.

6

America

⋄═○═⋄

The next morning it is as if David's proposal never happened. We talk excitedly about New York. We bundle up and David opens the promenade deck door. The wind is brisk but it's a beautiful sunny morning. We'll have a perfect view of our new country.

As the ship slows, we know we are close. Behind us, people push and jostle their way forward. David stands near me to keep others from blocking my view. "There she is!" someone yells from behind us.

Everyone falls silent. On an island in the middle of the harbor is a massive statue of a woman wearing a crown and holding a torch—the Statue of Liberty. As we pass by her, we see an American flag blowing in the wind. Tears stream down my face.

The steamer slows even more and other passengers begin to leave the deck to gather their baggage. David and I remain on the deck transfixed—I have not yet set foot on her soil, but I think I am already in love with America.

We dock at the Hudson River Pier. Immigration officials come on board and when one looks at my papers, he puts a mark at the top before he returns them to me. He tells me I will have to go with the steerage passengers back out to the island where the woman stands. I feel as though I will faint, and look at David, who is standing in another line. He is powerless to help me.

I am traveling alone and must determine, for myself, what to do. Though shaking in fear that I will be detained and sent back to Europe, I recover my breath. I will never see David again and yet all I can do is wave to him as I walk away.

⊷══◉◉══⊶

Tateh hands me the reins. He tells me it is time I learned how to drive the horse that pulls our wagon. The horse rears. The reins fly out of my hands and the horse begins to run, dragging us behind it. Some of Tateh's goods fall out of the wagon onto the road.

Finally, the horse comes to a stop and Tateh climbs down. He gathers the things that have fallen and retrieves the reins, then hands them back to me. "No, Tateh. I am afraid," I say and begin to cry.

"Boshka," he replies, "There will come many times in your life when you are afraid. In those moments, you must surrender your fear and go wherever it takes you, and trust that you have the strength to do what you must to survive."

⊷══◉◉══⊶

I gather my bags and, standing tall, move toward the ferry that will take me to a place called Ellis Island. I disembark with all of

36

the others and am directed to enter a large building. The "Receiving Hall," by far the biggest room I have ever seen, is packed with passengers from steerage. An immigration official quickly directs the few of us who traveled in first or second class into a smaller waiting room.

The inspector, pleasant and efficient but somewhat stern, motions for my documents and examines them. He looks at me and back at them, and I swallow hard. After a moment, he speaks in English.

When I don't respond, he asks in German, "When were you born?"

His eyes move to my breasts and I realize that he thinks because of my size I am younger than what the papers say. I answer his questions as quickly and confidently as I can, though my knees are shaking under my dress.

Finally, his demeanor changes and a more pleasant expression appears on his face. "Boshka," he says. "I'm afraid Boshka won't do in America."

I can relax now. I remember Miriam writing about this in one of her letters. Her name remained almost the same, but she said the Yiddish names of many of her friends were changed because Americans couldn't pronounce or spell them.

"We'll call you Elizabeth," he says. "You are now *Elizabeth Markman*." He says it slowly, as he writes my new name, where I'm from and the date—January 24, 1906—into a big book. He hands back the documents and says to me, "Welcome to America, Elizabeth, and good luck. You are free to go."

I say one of the few English phrases that I learned on the ship. "Thank you."

He nods and I put my papers into my valise. "E-liz-a-beth," I say, trying out my new name. It will take some getting used to.

Outside of the Receiving Hall, I freeze. I do not know where to go—I have no idea how to get back to where the carriages are. Seeing my distress, a woman with two little boys points to another ferry and tells me in Yiddish that it will take me to a place called Battery Park. There, she says, I can show a policeman the address and he will tell me what I must do to get there.

As I walk toward the ferry, I see men with clubs strapped to their sides. I take a step back and watch from a distance. Something is different here, however. Instead of threatening, these men answer questions, smile and gesture to the swarm of immigrants to go onto the ferry, and they are laughing and joking, without fear. I move forward, but when I do, I move as far as I can to the back of the ferry. Just in case.

On the ferry, I meet another Yiddish-speaking woman who is traveling, like David, to Chicago. She tells me that once we reach Battery Park, police will direct immigrants to trolleys, but that I should ask a policeman to help me look for a carriage.

"Are you sure that is safe?" I say, still nervous about the officers in uniform.

"Yes. The police in America are different."

I am still not convinced, but I tell her my name and ask that if she happens to meet a man named David in her travels to give him my regards and tell him I am fine. She promises that she will and resumes talking with her family.

As the ferry approaches Battery Park, my fear is replaced by wonder—after many months of dreaming, I am ready to begin a new life for myself. Once on dry land, I see that the buildings are even larger than they seemed from the ferry—I stare at them, modern and towering, and crane my neck as I try to count the floors of the tallest one.

Everything seems to move with a faster pace here. Throngs of people speaking Russian, Yiddish, German and a host of languages I cannot identify move quickly by—even women pushing prams are in a hurry.

I do not want to bring attention to the fact that I am a woman alone so I follow a group of people who were on the ferry. Before we have moved very far, I see carriages lined up and passengers climbing aboard. Listening for anyone who speaks a language I know, I hear an attractive, young couple conversing in German. I approach to ask their assistance, but before I can, they climb into a carriage, and I hurry to join them. The driver cracks his whip gently in the air and we begin to move.

I watch as other carriages and trolley cars and people on foot weave in and out of traffic on the paved streets. I think of our horses in Glubokoye that pull Tateh's wagon—and I'm sure, like me, they'd be frightened of all the commotion. The woman of the couple notices my wide eyes and leans over to speak. "This is Fifth Avenue," she says. "It's a very important street."

The carriage driver turns around and says something to me in English. I look at the woman and tell her I don't understand and she translates for me. "He wants to know if you're going to Yorkville."

"I am going to the Upper West Side," I reply.

She translates to the carriage driver. He shakes his head and stops the horses, then turns and gestures toward me.

"She needs to go to Broadway. Tell her to get off and find another carriage to Broadway. Sorry."

The woman explains this to me and points to the corner up ahead, repeating the word "Broadway." Bewildered, I step down onto the street and the driver hands me my bags. The Germans smile and wave to me from the carriage as it pulls away.

I am alone again, standing at the corner of Broadway and Fifth Avenue. Women in big fur coats and hats with feathers rush by. Men in funny-shaped hats hurry into buildings with glass doors. I hear whistles, people talking, boys selling newspapers, neighing horses, bells on the trolleys. New York is quite different from Vilna and Hamburg, and a world away from Glubokoye.

I feel a tap on my shoulder. "Pardon me, miss. Do you need help?"

It is a policeman. I have no idea what he's saying. He speaks again, this time in German. "Are you lost?"

I scan his smiling face and friendly eyes and nod. He doesn't seem to be angry so I take out the piece of paper with Lillian's address and hand it to him. "Here is where I am going."

He peers at the paper and points in the direction I am to go. "You need a carriage to go up Broadway. Let me get one for you."

I stare at him, still in disbelief, as he steps off the curb and into the street. After a few minutes, he comes back with a carriage and signals to me. "The driver speaks German," he says as he takes my bags from me and helps me into the carriage.

"*Danke,*" I say.

Within a few minutes, the view from the carriage begins to change. Now, instead of the tall buildings, I see street lamps and black wrought-iron fences that look like those in Vilna and Hamburg, but everything in New York is on a much grander scale, larger and more luxurious—even the streets are wider and sidewalks are everywhere.

"Where are you from?"

"Vilna, in Lithuania," I say. Maybe he will have heard of Vilna. Probably not Glubokoye.

"I've been there once. It's a beautiful place."

We ride along in silence for a few more blocks. "It is good that you are going to the Upper West Side," he says. "You are very fortunate. Those from the Pale who live on the Lower East Side are very poor. You will see for yourself, perhaps, but if you go there, do not go alone. Where you are going is a nice area. Lots of wealthy people live there in brownstones."

I pretend that I know what he is talking about. Though I have heard the word a number of times, I do not know what a "brownstone" looks like.

He points out the massive lions on the steps of the New York Public Library and then nods toward a large park. "That's Central Park. You should go there when you're settled."

We turn off Broadway onto a road named "72nd Street" and then again, this time down a road called "Columbus Avenue." Like the buildings near Battery Park, the houses we pass are larger than any I've ever seen. The driver pulls the horses to a stop, and I am sure that he has made a mistake. Tateh and Mamaleh told me that Lillian is rich but even they could not have imagined this.

7

❖─➣◉◖─❖

The house is made of rust-colored stones and is attached to other houses on either side of it. It has three floors and three large windows on each. I giggle to myself. So this is what "brownstone" means, I think. I have been in New York for only a few hours and already I have learned many things.

I pick up my bags and mount the stairs. A servant dressed in a black and white uniform opens the door. Before I can think what to say to her, the door opens wider and a tall slender woman with perfectly coiffed chestnut brown hair steps in front of her. "Boshka!" she cries.

My mouth drops. It is Lillian. I know it because she has Tateh's eyes. She is lovelier than I'd imagined. She places her hands on my shoulders and holds me away as if to inspect me. "Look at you, Boshka!" she says in Yiddish.

She looks me over again. This time her eyes fill with tears. "My baby sister is all grown up and beautiful," she says.

I hear the sound of heavy footsteps behind Lillian.

"Who is it?" a man's voice calls out.

"My sister Boshka has finally arrived. Isn't that wonderful?"

There is no reply.

Lillian shrugs. "Mr. Bechhofer can seem harsh at times, but he will love you as I do already. I am certain."

I sense something is wrong, but I don't know what it is. I step inside the house. A bouquet of flowers rests on a carved rosewood table in the hallway. I follow Lillian past rows of large paintings in gilt frames and into a living room with an enormous stone fireplace at one end. A mirror resembling an archway reflects the light, which is streaming through two large windows.

Lillian gestures for me to sit in a dark velvet chair trimmed in gold and within seconds, a servant tiptoes across the hardwood floor and sets a tea service on a small table. All I can think is that my sister has come a long way since Glubokoye. As if reading my mind, she hurries to explain. "My husband is a very successful cigar retailer with a head for business. And you know how men love their cigars these days. He just made a profitable business deal with some Cubans. They have the best cigars—I don't know why but they do."

We sit on the davenport sipping tea and eating dainty almond cookies. As she pours another cup of tea, she nearly upsets the table.

"Lillian, is it all right that I'm here?"

"Oh yes, of course! Of course! I am so clumsy sometimes." I watch her closely as she rearranges the tea and cookies. I do not think her clumsy at all.

After a while, Lillian's husband enters the room. He glares at me and I try to shrink into the davenport. Lillian quickly rises to her feet and approaches him. In English, the two exchange what seem to be harsh words, but Lillian doesn't translate. I know why soon enough.

The man turns to me and speaks in German. "We're having a party tonight. I'll show you to the kitchen. You can put on an apron and the other servants will show you what to do."

Numbly, I follow him into the kitchen where a young woman only slightly older than I hands me an apron and tells me I will wash dishes once the guests are served. I am caught off guard, but I quickly gather my wits. I turn to face Mr. Bechhofer, who is now standing in the doorway behind Lillian. I see his coldness, the harsh look on his face, the way she trembles when he is near. It dawns upon me that he agreed for me to live with them as a *servant*, not as a sister.

"I see you have brought me here to be a maid," I say to him. I toss the apron aside, though I want to throw it at his feet. "I will be glad to repay you for any expenses you may have incurred, but I am a dressmaker, not a maid."

It is his turn to be startled. Before he can respond, I turn to Lillian. "If you will help me gather my things, I will go on to Miriam and Lou Schaffer's. They are expecting me." I have no idea if Miriam and Lou are even home, but in my bravado, I want to be anywhere but where I am.

I can see that Lillian is disappointed but I can also see that she is proud of the way I have stood up to her husband. She calls for another servant to help me gather my things and I follow the woman upstairs to the guest room. I pick up my things and bundle up again for the cold. When I return to the front door, Lillian is waiting for me, dressed in a long fur coat.

"Lillian, you have the party to attend to…"

"No," she says, "you're a young lady by yourself getting into a carriage at night. It isn't proper. I'll walk you."

She quietly closes the door behind us as if to avoid notice and I can tell she has done this before. We walk a short distance up to a busier street. At night, New York is different—chillier and not so bustling—and I am glad she is with me.

Lillian puts out her hand to get the attention of the driver of a carriage coming up the street. I grab her other hand and say, "We'll meet in the city when your husband isn't around."

As I step into the carriage, she murmurs, "Boshka, please don't tell Tateh." I pause for a moment and then nod my head. Tateh isn't in America. There is nothing he can do for her. He must go on believing his Lillian is happy and that her husband is as kind to her as he is to Mamaleh.

Once settled in the carriage, I hand the driver the paper with Miriam and Lou's address and we move away from the curb. The street lamps glow and I shiver, wondering if I will find a warm place to sleep tonight. What if Miriam and Lou refuse to help me? Where will I go?

The adrenalin of the exchange with Lillian's husband wanes and I am suddenly too exhausted even to wonder what lies in store for me ahead. After what seems forever, the carriage arrives at a house that looks much like Lillian's. It is also a brownstone. Once again, I trudge up a set of steps and knock on the door. This time a young man answers.

He speaks to me in English. "May I help you?" I recognize this as a phrase I learned on the ship. "*Ja. Danke,*" I say.

He switches into German and invites me to step inside. I explain that I'm looking for Lou and Miriam Schaffer. "Oh, yes," he says, pointing up. "They live on the second floor. Here is the elevator," he says, pointing to an iron cage. "I'll alert them that you are here."

By the time I have moved myself and my things into the elevator, the young man returns. Stepping into the cage with me, he closes the door and presses a lever. We begin to rise. Massive buildings and now telephones and cages that go up and down—I can only shake my head.

When we stop, the young man helps me with my bags, and after knocking on the door to the apartment, he tips his cap to me and steps back onto the elevator. Within a few seconds, a man with dark hair and brown eyes answers the door and smiles broadly.

"Boshka, we're so glad you're here. Come in, come in," he says to me in Yiddish.

I am startled. "How do you know who I am?"

The man smiles again. "Your sister telephoned us to say you were on your way." He gazes at me, momentarily transfixed. Though it has been many years since I saw him last, Lou Schaffer looks remarkably the same.

Miriam runs across the room and throws her arms around me. "Boshka! Boshka! You're here, you're finally here! You must be starving! I'll have Yetta prepare a bedroom and set a place for you at the table before she leaves for home. The food is still warm, I'm sure. We had just begun dinner when Lillian telephoned."

When Miriam mentions food, I realize I am ravenous. Except for the cookies at Lillian's, I've had nothing to eat since breakfast on the ship. Miriam and Lou take me into the dining room and Yetta, a woman about Miriam's age sets a plate in front of me.

Once Yetta returns to the kitchen, Miriam explains that she works for them during the day and returns to her own family in the evening. "Yetta is from Russia. She is hardworking, kind, and pleasant, Boshka. I know you'll like her. And oh, how she can cook!"

I look down for the first time at my plate. I recognize slices of beef and boiled potatoes, but there are a number of foods that I cannot identify. I poke at them with my fork and Miriam giggles. "I've forgotten what it's like to eat American food for the first time."

Without thinking for a moment about whether it is kosher, I proceed to gobble down everything on my plate. Throughout the meal, Miriam quizzes me about everyone in Glubokoye, especially my family. She asks about the places where we used to play and friends from school. I am reminded that Miriam likes to talk and tonight, I am glad—it helps me not to worry about Lillian or what I am going to do.

Lou, on the other hand, quietly listens as his sister and I talk and he nods or mumbles something in support every now and then. He is not a talker like Miriam, but he does seem to be kind.

I tell Miriam and Lou that, despite traveling first class, I was required to go to Ellis Island and Lou asks if they gave me a new name. I nod and say the name given to me as best as I can. "E-liz-a-beth."

Miriam exclaims. "No, no, that won't do! It doesn't sound Jewish at all." She thinks for a moment. "I know! We'll call you 'Bessie.' It's short and popular among Russian women here. Yes, that's it! It is very American and Jewish too."

Miriam knows better than I do what is proper and what is not, but I admit I don't understand why a short name could be Jewish but not its longer version. There are so many things to learn about America.

"Well, then, Bessie Markman, I bet you are ready for bed! I'll show you to your room. There will be time enough to show you around the neighborhood tomorrow."

I look at Miriam and then at Lou. "So, it is all right for me to stay here with you for a little while?"

Lou nods and smiles. "Oh, yes, Bessie, you may stay as long as you like. We are happy to have you as our guest. You are family."

8

I wake the next morning with my head on Nathan's pillow. Already, I dread the day I'll have to find him and make good on my promise to his mother.

After dressing for breakfast, I emerge from the bedroom and explore the house. I discover that although it takes up the entire second floor of the brownstone, Lou and Miriam's home is neither as fancy nor as large as Lillian's. The furniture seems a bit worn, but it is more comfortable and the rooms have a warmer feel that matches the welcome with which I was received.

When I finally arrive in the dining room, I hear Yetta happily humming to herself. Lou is sitting at the table with a newspaper in one hand and a cup of coffee in the other.

"Good morning, Lou," I say, as cheerily as possible.

"Good morning, Bosh—I mean Bessie. You surprised me!" He sets his cup and paper on the table and jumps up to attend to my chair.

A moment later, Miriam joins us. "Good morning!" she says, in English.

I smile at her exuberance and respond in German. "*Guten morgen!*"

"No, Bessie, say it in English."

I mimic her as best I can and she smiles. "Good. You've a strong accent, but your pronunciation will come around." Unlike Lillian, Miriam seems able to shift easily from English to Yiddish. So does Lou—when he manages to get a word in.

I sit back and look at my friend. Miriam is pretty, but not beautiful like Lillian. Her energy, however, makes her very attractive. She has blond curls—once the envy of everyone in Glubokoye—and a heart-shaped face. Of medium height, she now has a farm woman's body, but when dressed in her American clothes, she is quite fashionable. I find myself wondering why she is still single.

Yetta appears from the kitchen with a tray and places a bowl of something in front of me. "Is this porridge?" I ask.

"Yes, but here it's called oatmeal."

Yetta brings out another plate, this one overflowing with fruit and bread. Miriam points at each of the foods and calls it by its English name.

Now I understand why she is so shapely. Americans eat well—and a lot.

Lou finishes his coffee and leaves for work. As soon as Miriam finishes eating and the dishes are removed from the table, she and I take a walk so she can show me the neighborhood. As we stroll along, she explains that she and Lou moved to Washington Heights because of the subway. "Wherever a subway station is built, there is usually a construction boom and people flock to live nearby," she says. "Many of the German-American Jews have moved to Washington Heights because of it. The station is almost ready for use."

I listen while Miriam chatters on, trying to take in all this new information and see everything at the same time. "Never go to Central Park alone at night. It's dangerous. And the Lower East Side, where all the Yiddish-speaking Jews live, is dangerous too. I'll take you there sometime, but only in daylight.

"The poverty there will break your heart," she says, "but that's where all of the Yiddish theaters and kosher restaurants are. Lou and I used to go fairly often but not so much anymore. It's filthy and too unsafe after dark."

Everywhere we go, Miriam greets people she knows in English. Many carry bags and bundles from doing their morning shopping. As we meander, we pass a candy store, a bookshop, a kosher butcher, a kosher restaurant, a lady's millinery shop and a men's haberdashery. Occasionally, policemen trot by on horseback.

"Because this is a mostly Jewish area," she says, "it's different from other parts of the city. In observation of the Sabbath, we stop work on Fridays before sundown. Many shops reopen on Sundays."

We walk for several more blocks and Miriam is uncharacteristically quiet. Finally, she breaks the silence. "I'm so glad you're here with us, Bessie. But would you mind telling me what happened with Lillian? I know Lazar Bechhofer has a reputation for being unpleasant."

I tell her the story. Miriam says she's not surprised, that Lillian's husband believes himself to be better than other people and that he is not known for his generosity. "Oh, Bessie," she says, "I'm so sorry you had to go through that. When we moved here, I tried to maintain contact with Lillian, but she keeps mostly to herself."

I shrugged my shoulders. "I wasn't sure what to do. It hurt me to leave her last night but even though I was frightened, I could not stay. My parents will know something is not right when I write them that I am here with you and Lou. Tateh will be very disappointed."

For a moment, Miriam is silent. "Perhaps Lillian will come to her senses one day and leave him. Such a beautiful woman—in her time, many nice men with money would have married her. But she made her choices, and only she can change them."

I saw my opportunity. "Miriam, may I ask a question of you?"

"Yes, of course."

"Why have neither you nor Lou married?"

"Well, I haven't found the right man yet. I guess I've been too busy helping Lou with the company books and doing charity work—I'm chairwoman of the hospital fundraiser this year. Don't worry, Bessie—I'll find a good Jewish man one day and he'll take care of me.

"And as for Lou, well, no woman has ever been good enough for him." She looks at me with a twinkle in her eye.

9

⋆⇒◉⇐⋆

I've been here for a month now, and I've been unable to find a job in Washington Heights. Any job requires I speak English well. Miriam and Lou have tried to help me secure a dressmaking job. They have asked their friends, but unless I have special skills, there is no work except in the factories located on the Lower East Side.

Today, Miriam is having friends for the afternoon, but I am more interested in looking for a job than sitting in the parlor and listening to gossip, so I excuse myself. I tell her I will venture out to explore New York on my own, and she suggests I get a carriage to drive me around Central Park. I nod, but as soon as I leave the house, I go straight to the trolley stop. I have decided to go to the Lower East Side and apply for one of the factory jobs.

I am nervous—I remember the carriage driver's warning. I notice a Yiddish newspaper on the seat on the trolley. I pick it up and I read: "Wanted: Healthy, industrious girls and women to sew ladies garments. Apply at the Schweitzer Factory."

I memorize the address and tell the trolley conductor to let me off at the Lower East Side. He looks at me strangely and then nods. I think perhaps there is something wrong with how I look and then remember that young ladies from Washington Heights don't often take trolleys to the Lower East Side, especially alone.

The trolley bumps along, picking up more and more immigrants as we travel along. The car becomes a babble of languages from English to Russian to German to languages I don't recognize and I am fascinated. These people are different from those I remember in Vilna and Hamburg.

I smooth a wrinkle in my dress and notice that my clothes have grown tighter from all the food at Miriam and Lou's. And on my walks in Central Park, I have discovered the street vendors selling Hebrew National sausage rolls. They are quite tasty and best of all, they are kosher. Tateh and Mamaleh would be proud that I have not eaten treif since I arrived.

After a long ride the driver motions that we have reached my stop. When I step off the trolley onto 14th Street, the stench overwhelms me and I gasp for air. I see nothing but dirty faces and tattered clothes, and I remember the poorest area of Glubokoye where Tateh and I sometimes delivered bread to the needy.

Laundry hangs from every fire escape and some children run barefooted. I cringe each time I see them stepping in the filth of urine and feces left by the horses. I pass fruit and vegetable vendors selling their food like in the markets in the old country. Wearing a new wool coat Miriam bought me as a present—she insisted that cloaks like mine are not fashionable in America—I begin to think I am conspicuous.

I see a policeman and I find I am not as afraid as only a month ago. I ask him for directions to the Schweitzer factory and like the trolley conductor, he also looks at me with an odd expression. "It's down that street—two blocks—and around the corner to the left. A large red brick building—you'll see it right away, miss."

When I arrive at the factory, I am directed to a tall, officious German, who blusters at me when, without thinking, I answer his first question in Yiddish. "You'll speak in German if you want a job here. Be here at seven in the morning—sharp. If you are late, you will not be allowed to enter."

I am hired! I'm on my way to being a working woman in America but a pit forms in my stomach. I walk quickly back to the trolley stop at 14th Street, retracing my steps from the directions the policeman gave me. When I come into the apartment, Miriam's busy at work on the books for Lou's wholesale coffee and tea business. I hurry to my room to wash off all signs of the filth of the Lower East Side before she notices.

I come out when I hear Lou open the door. I listen as he greets Miriam, who doesn't immediately respond. He speaks to her again. "Shhhh, this is very complicated," she says.

I think of Tateh. He used to trust me to write down each day's sales and receipts in the ledger book. I attempt to act as if I hadn't overheard their conversation when I enter the living room. Miriam asks me if I've had a pleasant afternoon.

"Lou, Bessie went out all by herself for a carriage ride all around Central Park." I am petrified that she will ask me about the park—I am not ready to tell them about the job but I won't lie.

Fortunately, Yetta soon appears from the kitchen to announce that dinner is served.

During the meal, Miriam chatters on and on about the ladies who came to tea, describing what they wore, telling us all the gossip. I ask many questions to stop her from asking about my afternoon. At the slightest pause, I grow more fearful until finally I can't bear it another minute and excuse myself from the table on the pretense of a headache. Except that it isn't a pretense—the tension and worry has made my head throb.

Morning comes and I dress as quietly as possible so as not to disturb Miriam and Lou, tiptoeing out of the house even before Yetta appears. I'm beginning to feel like a real New Yorker—after my trolley ride yesterday, I know how to pay the fare and now understand at least some of the driver's English. Miriam refuses to speak Yiddish with me so my English is improving.

Miriam is fun and popular and my dearest friend, but the life she has is not the one I want. She shops in the morning, has lunch with her friends and then does what she calls "charity work"—which mostly consists of ladies coming to the house for tea, sandwiches and gossip just like yesterday afternoon. When I told her that I didn't want Lou to continue supporting me, she laughed and said, "He doesn't care. And besides, if you would marry him, his fortune would be half yours." She smiles at her own joke.

Miriam has developed that American directness that I sometimes admire yet find annoying at other times. I am not looking for a husband! And if I were, I don't see Lou that way. He is my friend!

When I arrive at the factory, a line of women has already formed at the entrance to the building. I stand in the back and listen to Yiddish and it makes me feel at home. A few of the women stare at me, but no one speaks. Once in the building, we all trudge up six flights of stairs. By the time we reach the top, I'm sweating, and I know why the others took off their coats and shawls at the entrance.

The door opens and each woman walks to an assigned place. My mouth falls open—hundreds hunch over sewing machines while their feet move up and down on treadles. Unfinished garments are piled next to each.

The floor is covered with scraps of cloth and thread. The room is dark—the glass in the large windows is so dirty, very little light comes in. A few electric bulbs hang by worn cords from the ceiling. I start to feel cold again without my coat and realize the room is unheated.

Men roam the factory floor, watching the women sew. After a moment, one of them comes up to me. "You're new, yes?"

"Yes, I'm Bessie Markman."

"Follow me," he commands, and leads me to a seat in the corner. He gestures for me to sit down and hands me a card. "Put your information on here. The pay is $8 a week. We work a 10-hour workday, from seven to six, Monday through Saturday."

I am shocked. He is obviously Jewish. "We work on the Sabbath?"

He responds by repeating the litany of information.

Something else is wrong—7 a.m. to 6 p.m. is *eleven* hours, not ten. My mind flashes back to something Lou read in the newspapers. It is illegal for factories to make women work more than ten hours a day, but many owners disobey the law.

The man seems to read my thoughts. "It takes time for you to get up here from the street, time for you to go to the toilet, time for you to eat lunch, time for you to receive your wages. That is why you will be here at the factory for eleven hours. Ten hours for work. One hour for not working.

"The woman next to you will explain further—you must sew the pile of garments we give you by day's end. No exceptions. You sew, we pay. You will receive your wages once a week—on Saturday, at the end of the day."

He walks away and I turn to the woman next to me. "Hello," I say. "My name is Bessie."

She doesn't look up. Though she can't be much older than I am, she is like an old woman—frail and sickly.

"Pardon me," I say again. "My name is Bessie."

She mumbles in Yiddish, "Take off that fancy coat."

I immediately obey.

Head still down, she continues to talk to me. "Don't wear that to work again or you'll be robbed on the way out of here. At six o'clock, roll your coat into a ball and carry it with you to the trolley. Don't put it back on until you get to wherever you came from." She works the treadle on her machine, pushes cloth under the needle and speaks all at the same time, stopping only to cough.

I tell her my name again.

She clenches her teeth. "Listen carefully to what I say. We are not people here—we are numbers. I am number 204. You are number 205." After another spasm of coughing, she continues. "What matters is that you finish your sewing at the end of the day and you do it well. These German Jews inspect everything we do. Don't be too good or too fast at your sewing, because there is no reward for it. The faster you sew, the more they will give you to do. Improve a little bit every few weeks or so. That will keep them happy."

I am in shock. Since the day I began dreaming of America, I have been designing clothes in my head, yet here I am, little more than a slave. My nerves are already on edge when a loud boom is heard. In concert, the overseers have slammed the doors shut and locked them.

I look questioningly at Number 204. "It is to prevent us from stealing," she whispers, never stopping. "Now, stop talking and watch how I operate this machine. Then you try." She coughs again.

She shows me how to thread the needle and put the cloth in place. Her feet operate the treadle as she moves the garment around. It looks easy.

"Now you try on your machine."

I thread the needle, and though it takes me a few minutes, I put the garment in place and start moving the treadle with my feet. Yes, it's easy.

"No, no! What are you doing? You can't sew anywhere you'd like. Follow the seams in the pattern. You just sewed across a sleeve." She sighs. "Pull out the stitching and begin again."

I try to lift the stitches with my fingernails. She hands me a silver, U-shaped instrument that comes to a sharp point at both ends. I hold it up closer to the light above us. She leans over. "Your father must've been useful in the Pale. Look at those hands—like a newborn babe's. That will change."

She shows me how to reach under stitches to take them out and glances at two men who have been watching us from the beginning. "Hurry. The Germans don't like mistakes."

I remove the stitches as quickly as possible and re-sew the sleeve, more slowly this time. Number 204 checks my work and nods her approval. I put my head down and start sewing again. Tears roll down my cheeks and I stop to wipe my eyes with my sleeve.

"205!" I close my eyes and try not to cry. My teacher admonishes me to get to work and then says nothing more.

At midday, while still at their seats, the workers stuff food in their mouths. I hadn't thought to bring food and near the end of the day, I am famished. I think that between hunger and work, this has been the longest day of my life. My ankles hurt from working the treadle, my fingers bleed from threading the needle and I desperately need a toilet. I vow to myself I will never drink two cups of coffee before coming to work again.

At six o'clock, one of the Germans walks to the center of the room and rings a bell. Everyone around me stops sewing.

The Germans spread out and inspect our work. I hold my breath as one of them comes down the line to me. I have finished my pile but I am unsure that my work is correct. He examines the garments and nods that I can leave.

Once out on the street again, I try not to breathe in the air. I hold my coat in my hands, balled up as "204" instructed me. My whole body shakes.

I feel a tap on my shoulder. It is "204." "Here, wear this," she mumbles, and hands me a knitted sweater. "You'll get very cold on the trolley. I don't live very far. You can bring it back tomorrow." She's coughing so badly I can hardly understand her.

I start to protest and then thank her. "What is your name? Where do you live?"

She is already walking away but stops and turns back. "My name is Rachael." She points to a building not far away. "I live there, so I don't need the sweater." She turns and hurries away. I hope she heard me thank her.

A cascade of thoughts fills my head as I walk to the trolley. Fueled by the sights and sounds and putrid smells, I feel ashamed at how consumed I have been with myself. My stomach growls, but unlike most of the people I see, I will not go hungry tonight.

How could I have been so uncaring, so oblivious of the poor—on the ship, in Hamburg, in Vilna? I had hardly even noticed them in Glubokoye. My thoughts turn to Rachael. How sick she seems! What if she gets worse? What if she has children? How will she care for them?

I think of where I am going and the warmth of the house in Washington Heights, and I'm saddened. America is supposed to have streets of gold yet what I see here is ugly and tarnished.

I trudge, cold and hungry, to the trolley stop. By the time I climb on, all the seats have been taken and I have to stand, hanging on to a strap with only my fingers. I'm so tired I must concentrate so as not to lose my grip and fall. When finally Washington Heights comes into view, my knees are buckling beneath me.

As I reach to unlock the door, Miriam throws it open. "Oh, Bessie, where have you been? We've been so worried about you. When you weren't in your room this morning, we couldn't imagine what had happened to you."

She looks down at my hands. From the look on her face I realize I'm still holding my coat in a ball—I forgot to switch back on the way from the trolley.

"Bessie, where did you get that shmata? Why aren't you wearing the coat I bought you?"

I know I am caught so I explain about the job but try not to tell her how horrible it was. She starts to scold me but I begin to cry, and the expression on her face softens. She calls to Yetta to bring me warm soup and then scans me up and down. A look of concern now appears on her face. I politely brush her off because I'm too tired to talk anymore.

After two bowls of soup, I walk into the living room and slump onto the couch. Lou is reading a newspaper but puts it down when I enter. "Bessie, I'm sorry you had such a hard day. Please let me help you. I'm sure you'll be able to find a better job. Don't go back to the factory—I've told you you're welcome to stay here with us. You don't need to work—you're not a burden at all."

I smile as warmly as I can. "I know that, Lou. And I will definitely think about it."

I realize it's a lie. I won't. They don't—no, that's wrong, they *can't* understand what I feel. It's important that I make a way for myself and I will do whatever it takes.

I close my eyes, and the next thing I know, Miriam is tapping me on the shoulder. "Bessie, darling, let's get you into bed."

Once in my room, I think about Rachael and picture the building she pointed to. I sink into the bath Yetta has drawn for me and then crawl into bed, grateful for the warm quilts.

I wake at five a.m. so I'll have plenty of time to eat a huge breakfast. I am careful to remember to drink just one cup of coffee. I search through my clothes for something plain to wear—I have nothing as shabby as Rachael or the rest of the factory girls. I pull my hair into a loose bun on top of my head, comb through the clothes in my closet to find my cloak and stuff bread and a piece of fruit into its pockets.

I am almost out the door when I remember Rachael's sweater, and I return to my room. As I leave, the pretty embroidery on Nathan Dreizen's pillow catches my eye and I pause to read its message again. *May this pillow bring you peace.* I am consoled for the moment, strengthened even, and decide Mr. Dreizen will have to wait a little while longer.

I tiptoe downstairs to avoid Miriam and Lou and rush to the trolley. As I literally run, I realize I'm hurrying to a second day of misery. But I keep going—I can't be dependent on Lou, or any man, for security.

At the factory, my heart sinks even further when I see that Rachael isn't there—a new girl has taken her place. I take off my cloak and start to work. Within minutes a gruff German woman is standing over me, glaring. "Number 205," she barks, "your sewing is wrong. Fix it. Make no more mistakes. Do you understand?"

I nod and take out the stitches—in my haste, I've sewn across a sleeve again. I am finding it difficult to concentrate and the dragging of time makes it worse. I slip a piece of bread from my pocket and nibble at it. Perhaps eating will help.

The woman is back. "This work is unacceptable. Now you've sewn through the cuff of this garment." I hear laughter behind me and I realize they are laughing at me.

"Please, God," I whisper under my breath. "Don't let me cry in front of these people. Help me to be brave."

"Pick up your things and leave immediately. You are no longer needed at this factory." The laughter stops abruptly and people return to work. I stare at the woman, and she repeats her command, this time pointing to the door.

I stumble from my chair, grab my cloak and head to the stairs, where I am humiliated again—I can't escape because the door is locked and I must wait until the matron arrives to open it. Once it is unlocked, I bolt through the door and run down the six flights of stairs.

When I am out on the street again, I realize I am clutching Rachael's sweater, but I am not in the mood to remain any longer than I have to on the Lower East Side, so I will have to return it some other way. Still fuming, I climb onto the trolley, and realize I am screaming in my head.

I will not be locked up in such a room again, I will not be treated with disrespect no matter how little money I have, I will not be a slave!

10

◆━◎━◆

March 7, 1906

Dear Tateh and Mamaleh,

I'm doing well. Life is good. I'm safe and happy.

I lay the pen down on the desk. They don't know I am living with Miriam and Lou. I sigh and pick up the pen again.

When I first arrived here, I discovered Lillian and Mr. Bechhofer are extremely busy. He is quite a successful businessman and provides Lillian with more than she'll ever need. Lillian's life is full with her duties in running the house and with all the parties and social functions she attends.

She and I decided it would be best that I live with Miriam and Lou. I am there now. They're treating me well—like family. Lou is quite successful just like Mr. Bechhofer and Miriam continues to search for a husband who will take care of her.

I tell them about all the good things New York has to offer, but I don't mention the poverty I've seen or my experience at the factory. I pretend the cruel bosses and terrible working conditions on the Lower East Side don't exist.

Tell Max and Jack they would enjoy Central Park. It's my new favorite place.

These days, I go to Central Park often and walk around in the snow. Miriam sometimes comes with me and we chat and watch the children sled down the hills or throw snowballs at each other. Children of all nationalities, races, and religions are playing in the park, watched over by parents or nursemaids. I see none of the taunting of Jewish children that I saw in Glubokoye. I can't help but smile.

But a minute later, I'm sad again. Even in America, we separate into our own disparate groups—me with the Jews, the others with their own kind, only meeting in passing. The children are all there, but they rarely play together.

My thoughts jump to Lillian. I've tried to contact her but to no avail. I hoped she would try to meet me—but it seems she's a prisoner in her own home. Not telling my parents the truth goes against the way they raised me to be, but I'm learning that sometimes a sin of omission is kinder, as there is nothing Tateh and Mamaleh can do.

I sign my name, fold the letter and insert it in the envelope and then seal it and pen the address. I will post it on Monday.

Since I've been here, I have learned that Miriam and Lou observe the Sabbath but in their own way, and I usually join them. Sometimes we venture outside and visit with Miriam's friends and at others, we walk around the neighborhood while Lou reads. Once in a while, we visit the synagogue.

Back home, the Sabbath is treated as sacred—with prayers, a close community, and traditional meals. Here in America, so many like Lou work such long hours, they're exhausted by the week's end and have little energy left for services.

But not everything is different. Men and women worship separately, just as at home—the men sit together, and the women also.

The first time I went with Miriam, I encountered the yentas I met on the ship. "Child, where have you been?" said one. "We've been asking around about you."

"My *name* is Bessie," I replied.

Their eyes narrowed at my curt response. "You're living well, I see," said one.

"Yes," I replied, gesturing toward Miriam, "Lou and Miriam Schaffer have been very kind to allow me to live with them, but now I'm looking for a job. If you hear of one, please let me know."

Upon hearing that I want to work, their demeanors changed. I'm sure they'll no longer want to associate with me—one of the "useful" Jews they talked about so disrespectfully. They believe anyone who works, especially with their hands, is beneath them, and that I should find a husband to take care of me like they have.

"You must visit us sometime," they said.

But they didn't mean it. When I saw them next, they waved hello but kept walking. It hurt my feelings at first, but now it suits me fine.

⋆⊷◉⊶⋆

It is Sunday afternoon and I am returning from a walk in the park when Miriam swings open the door to greet me. There is a big smile on her face.

I tease her. "What is it? Did you find a rich Jewish suitor?"

She laughs. "No, no. It's good news for *you*, Bessie. Lou found a job for you at the millinery shop right here in the neighborhood. He knows Mrs. Rosen and he spoke to her already. She needs someone to help her. He told her you would be perfect and she wants to meet you."

I have passed by the millinery shop in Washington Heights many times but have never been inside. "Mrs. Rosen…I met her with you one day, didn't I?"

"Yes, on one of our Sunday calls. Bessie, it's a perfect job for a woman if she must have one, but…" She stopped short.

"But what?"

"But you *do* have another choice. You *could* marry Lou. The way he looks at you…" She tilts her head down and to the side and watches me closely, pressing her lips together to suppress her frustration.

When I don't answer, she continues. "I just don't understand you. Lou's the best man I know. We would finally be real sisters! It would be perfect! We could go together to Central Park every day and you could join my lunches and help me plan charity events!"

She is right—though she *is* my best friend, she *doesn't* understand. "You know I love Lou, but not in that way. I do appreciate him speaking to Mrs. Rosen on my behalf. I will go and talk with her tomorrow."

I turn the conversation away from Lou. "Since you seem to want to discuss marriage, we should talk about Mr. Silverstein who lives in

68

the brownstone two doors down. The way he looks at *you*—now that's something to talk about."

She stares at me and I pretend to ignore her expression. "And that is not to mention the fact that he's wealthy and has the finest tailoring business in Washington Heights. Or that his family has a clothing supply business somewhere in the South."

"Bessie, he's not my type."

"He *is* your type. He's rich, he adores you. What more do you want?"

"The same is true about Lou, you know. Since you arrived at our door, there has been no other woman but you."

Her last statement makes me uncomfortable. "Miriam, I love you both dearly, but I'm not ready to settle into that life. At least not yet. I don't know for sure what I want, but I know what I *don't* want. Security and comfort are very important to me, but that's not enough. Somehow, I need to be a part of making it happen. It's confusing."

I guess it was just as confusing to her, because the conversation ended there. But I learn that she took my suggestion to heart because two weeks later, on a Sunday afternoon, I answer the door to find Mr. Silverstein standing in front of me. "I am here for Miriam," he says.

Before I can turn around, dressed in her finest, she struts past me and heads out the door, pausing only to turn back and wink at me. It is all I can do to get the door closed before I burst out laughing.

"At last, that woman has a suitor," yells Lou from the living room after they are out of earshot. He is oblivious to the scene that has just played out in the foyer, which makes me laugh even harder.

The next Monday I begin working at the millinery shop. Mrs. Rosen is a kind lady. Sometimes she brings in delicious pastries for us to share. I have long since stopped asking if they're kosher because I know Mrs. Rosen wouldn't eat them if they weren't.

My English is much improved and I find I enjoy selling hats to the ladies who come into the shop. I seem to have a talent for showing them which styles look best with their blue eyes or their brown hair or the lovely dress they're wearing. I take time to help them arrange a hat in the most becoming way and never encourage a lady to buy a hat that doesn't look good. I learned that from Tateh—he was adamant that his customers be treated as well as he expects to be treated. It all seems to be working—Mrs. Rosen says she's selling more hats than ever before now that I'm her best salesgirl. While it is true, it's also a joke—I'm her *only* salesgirl.

I have been at Mrs. Rosen's for a couple of weeks when on Sunday, Lou and Miriam each go out for the afternoon. I am at home alone straightening my room when I see Rachael's sweater. It's been two months since I was fired at the factory. I need to return the sweater and I decide to do it today instead of walking in the park.

I go to the kitchen and get some bread, fresh fruit and some cheese and stuff it all into a bag—I know Lou and Miriam won't care about the food. I fold the sweater neatly and place it on top and then change into my plainest clothes before hurrying around the corner to the trolley stop.

When the trolley reaches the Lower East Side, I get off and walk toward the factory. I think if I stand where Rachael gave me the sweater, I will be able to find the building where she lives. I notice as I walk, I am still forced to step around puddles and excrement from the horses that pull the wagons. Everywhere the eye can see, there is filth beyond imagination. I hoped things would be cleaned up by now, but I guess this is how things are all the time. Because I'm not rushing today, I see even more.

I continue past tramps nudged against one another for warmth and people buying stale bread from pushcarts in the street, and enter "The Bend." I've learned that this is a nickname for the southwestern end of Mulberry Street where the least fortunate Jews live. It's easy to tell when I am there—the signs are all now in Yiddish. Though I am repulsed by what I see, a part of me relaxes—I do not have to work so hard to communicate here.

I turn down another street and read a sign advertising food at a "two-cent, all-night" restaurant. Wooden carts of rotting fruits and vegetables line the street. Another sign reads "7 cent Lodging House." I can only imagine the accommodations inside.

I pass a cluster of pushcart vendors and realize I'm hungry. Taking a chance, I stop to buy a Hebrew National sausage roll from one of the vendors. I think about how wonderful it is that an immigrant could start his very own company in America, even in circumstances as horrid as these. Even though it is just a little pushcart, it is his business. He is his own boss.

He reminds me how out of place I must look because, as he hands me the roll, he leans close to me and speaks in a low voice. "Be careful of who you talk to," he whispers. "There is much illness in the Tenth Ward—typhus and smallpox are everywhere. Worst of all, though, is the wasting disease. People are dying from it. The undertakers pass through these neighborhoods every day."

I think of a time when, while riding through Central Park, Miriam and I came upon a hollow-eyed child who was coughing nonstop.

She told me that the child had "consumption" or what Mamaleh would have called "wasting disease." Perhaps I am fortunate to have been fired from the factory on my second day.

The push cart vendor continues to talk. I am eager to learn what he has to say so I nod in response. "It isn't just illness, however. If they don't die from typhus or smallpox, they starve to death." His voice drops to a whisper again. "Some have reached such states of despair that they have killed themselves and their families to spare themselves from misery. You can see why. They see no way out."

His eyes dart around as if to make sure no one else is listening. "My neighbors died last year—the husband gave poison to his sick wife and his little son and then took it himself. Life was just too hard."

I can't find words, so I change the subject and ask about the dance halls I see everywhere. "Why there are so many? There seems to be one on every block."

"Oh, those," he laughs. "Young people love to dance after a hard day's work—the Fox Trot is all the new rage. Then, sometimes, men go alone…to find…" He pauses, afraid it will offend me. I gesture for him to continue.

"Well, let me just say that *some* dance halls are not nice places, especially late in the evening. Those who drink too much beer can become very rough and loud. Many times there are fights and the police come. And then in some, men are charged to dance…with girls they do not know." He searches my face for signs that I know what he means. I think I do, though I try not to show it.

A new customer walks up. I thank the vendor for taking the time to talk to me. I walk toward the factory to the place where

Rachael gave me her sweater. I look around until I am sure I have located the building she pointed to and head in that direction.

When I reach the door and go in, I see that the lobby is dirty and in disrepair. I wait until a boy appears from upstairs and I speak to him.

"Excuse me, can you tell me the apartment where Rachael lives?" The boy's expression changes as he shows two fingers and points up the stairs.

I take great care as I climb. With each step, I hear a creak and feel the staircase shift. There is much noise—loud voices, babies crying. It feels colder inside the building than out yet the air is stifling and I find it difficult to breathe.

When I reach the door, I knock softly and a gaunt, sallow-faced man answers. "What do you want?"

"I'm looking for a woman named Rachael. She lent me her sweater and I am here to return it."

He looks me up and down. "I am Ezra, Rachael's husband. I am sorry you have come all this way, but I'm afraid my wife no longer needs the sweater. She died a month ago." The pain on his face is unmistakable, and I feel as if a horse has kicked me in the stomach.

"You are welcome to come in if you'd like," he continues, and despite some measure of fear, I feel obligated to step inside. I am unprepared for what I see. The room is filled with women of all ages—even young girls—who are sewing. Two small boys sit on the floor playing with an old cardboard box and scraps of cloth. The walls are black with soot from the fire and the ventilation is poor.

When my eyes adjust, I make out a woman in the far corner. She has a baby at her breast, and I blush—I should not be in a room with a man I do not know when a woman is nursing her child. Out of the corner of my eye, I notice a small kitchen with a wood stove. I realize there are only three rooms for all of these people.

I hand Ezra the bag, telling him it contains food and Rachael's sweater. At first he refuses the food, but I insist. "For the children," I say, and he finally concedes. Though he is beaten down by grief, I can tell he is kind like Tateh. He sees me to the door and closes it behind me.

⋅—◉◉—⋅

I gather the courage to tell Tateh the truth. "I know about the Czar and the terrible things he has done to us," I say. "But I still don't understand why you gave up something you loved to become a merchant. Rabbis are good men. Why does God allow such suffering?"

There is a hint of sadness in Tateh's eyes. He gently brushes my cheek with the back of his hand. "Boshka," he says, "God does not promise that life will be easy. Righteousness is not about what we do. It is about how we do it, how we treat others. Not even the Czar can change that."

⋅—◉◉—⋅

I return from the Lower East Side, but don't tell Miriam or Lou where I've been. I'm struggling to understand why I am so disturbed. I keep telling myself that I didn't really know Rachael—after all, I was with her for only a day. And yet, I can't get her out of my mind.

Since Sunday, I've been coming home after work and going straight to my room to lie down. I haven't felt much like making idle conversation at dinner, so Yetta has been bringing a tray to me. Miriam

74

and Lou know something is troubling me—I can tell by how careful Miriam is around me.

On Thursday, I come in from the shop and am headed to my room when Miriam stops me. "Bessie, Lou and I are worried about you. Are you okay? Has something happened?"

"No, Miriam. I am fine," I say. "I just think every day how lucky I am to have had you and Lou to come to. And then I think of the people on the Lower East Side, people like Rachael and her husband and their children. We should be helping people like them more. They're our people too."

"I don't understand. Has something changed?"

I decide it's time I confess that I went to the Bend, so I go into the parlor and signal for Miriam to join me. I tell her about Rachael, about the filth and sickness. I tell her what the street vendor said about his neighbor, that people are killing themselves in their despair. "I should've done more, Miriam. I should have gone to Rachael's the day I was fired from the factory, but I didn't. Instead, I got out of there as soon as I could. And that's just it—I *could* escape. Unlike Rachael."

Miriam seems almost relieved. "We were worried that something had happened—in the park or at Mrs. Rosen's." She pauses. "Bessie, there's nothing you could have done. It isn't your fault that Rachael had consumption. People are dying of it, even around here."

"I could have done *something*," I say, tears running down my face. "Miriam, the day this woman met me, she gave me her sweater! She didn't even know me but because she knew I might be cold or in danger walking home, she removed what was probably the warmest thing she owned and gave it to me! She was the one who was sick, yet she took care of me—the least I could have done was return the favor. I should have gone back sooner. I should have done something, if for no other reason than to let her know how grateful I was for her kindness. What would Tateh think of me?"

"He would think nothing bad of what you did, Bessie," she says in a muted voice. "He would say it is God's will. It was her time to die, and God took her."

I look at her in surprise and anger rises up from somewhere deep inside me. "I'm sorry, but I don't believe that, Miriam. I don't believe that Tateh would say that and I don't believe that for a woman with small children to die is God's will. No one should have to live like that. No one."

11

⊷⇒○⊂⇢

It's now April and the flowers are beginning to bloom. Though I missed Tateh and Mamaleh terribly, especially during Hanukkah, my first winter here was uneventful. It was very cold in New York but the white snow in Central Park was spectacular when viewed against the skyline of the city. With all the walking I've done, both to the park and to the new subway station on the west side, I've lost some weight—my dresses fit better now.

Miriam and Simon are spending a lot of time with each other these days. I don't fault Simon at all, but I cringe anew every time he sends a new hat or dress to Miriam. It makes her happy but seems so frivolous to me—especially since I've seen the reality of the way some people have to live.

In America, it seems that material things are more important than in the Pale. I suppose that's because even the wealthiest Jews in Europe aren't spared the anxiety of wondering when the violence shown against their less fortunate neighbors will reach them or when someone they know is taken away, never to return. Money is only something to keep pain at arm's length for as long as they can afford to pay the bribes demanded of them.

Here, though, having material things shows status and power. Getting it and trying to get more and more hardens one. Like Lillian's husband, for instance.

In any case, the way the rich women in Washington Heights gawk over dresses from Paris or velvet draperies offends me. I realize that I am much more like them than Rachael, but I know too that I can be happy without buying a new dress every week and I don't care a thing for expensive jewelry.

When Simon comes for dinner, Miriam goes on and on about the flowers and chocolate he brings her, the jewels and clothing he has showered on her and I often drift away, lost in my own thoughts. I think of Rachael's children without a mother and I am sad. The lives of men like Ezra and Simon are an ocean apart.

After many invitations, Miriam has agreed to visit Simon's family in New Orleans, where his family's clothing supply business is located. Simon will remain in New York, while Miriam takes the train alone. She will stay three weeks.

One evening after dinner, Lou and Simon retire to the parlor, leaving Miriam and me at the table. As soon as they're out of earshot, she leans over to me, all excited. "Bessie, I want you to leave your job at the millinery store and come with me to New Orleans!"

"You know I can't do that. Mrs. Rosen has come to depend upon me. Besides, I've started sending money back home to Tateh and Mamaleh and I want to send as much as I can."

Miriam pouts for a moment, but in the end, she stops pressuring me. She knows I am stubborn but she knows too that if Simon asks her to marry him, and she moves into his townhouse, it will be frowned on for me to live with Lou and not be married to him.

In the next afternoon's mail, there is a letter from Tateh and Mamaleh in the box for me. It has been weeks since I have heard from them and I rip it open, anxious to hear how things are in Glubokoye.

⊷═◉═⊶

Dear Boshka,

We are happy that you are doing well. New York sounds like a magical place, especially the park. You are a good sister for giving Lillian and Lazar time alone. They are a young couple and perhaps want to have a family soon.

We ran into Mrs. Dreizen yesterday...

⊷═◉═⊶

I stop reading. I've forgotten all about taking the pillow to Nathan. I've grown attached to it—since I've been in America, it has been my source of comfort sometimes—and I'm still not ready to give it up. Not yet.

I hope I'm not being selfish.

It's mid-June and it's beautiful—the sky is the blue of a robin's egg. I am in such a good mood that I hop on the trolley and ride to the park to watch the children and families. A refreshing breeze greets my face and I take a deep breath, inhaling the delicious smells of grass, trees and flowers. My mind wanders to the meadows of Glubokoye, where my family and I would have picnics by the lake.

I smile at the memory, but I don't cry. I'm not as emotional when I think about my family now. I still miss them terribly, but I realize it's their choice to stay in the Pale. Tateh and Mamaleh say they will die there and I have accepted that as fact. I'm saving up money for Max, though—hopefully by next year I can pay to bring him over.

I'm strolling near the entrance to the park when I hear my name. I look up to find Miriam waving at me and I walk to meet her. "I was hoping I'd find you here. Yetta made us a small picnic," she says, pointing to a basket.

"That sounds wonderful."

We walk to a nearby spot under a tree. Miriam takes out a thin sheet and spreads it on the grass. We sit and eat some of my new favorite foods—rye bread with a spread of chopped herring with egg and onion mixed in.

"We're spoiling our dinner," I say, as I lick my fingers.

"Oh well, we'll just eat *two* dinners today," she says, giggling. We continue to devour the contents of the basket and talk about the people we see. Finally, Miriam stops. Her expression is serious and my heart jumps into my throat. "Bessie," she says, "the truth is I came to the park because I need to talk to you."

"About what?"

She pauses dramatically, and then blurts it out. "Our engagement is official!" She sticks out her hand. An enormous diamond stares back at me.

I can't believe I didn't notice.

"Simon must love you very much."

She smiles wistfully. "Bessie, I think he does."

"And do you love him?"

"I do. And I'm growing to love him more and more. Oh, Bessie, he took me to the finest French restaurant in the city and promised me a mansion and lots of children!"

"I'm so happy for you but I don't understand. Why the sad face?"

"Because the mansion he promised me is in New Orleans. We're leaving immediately after the wedding."

All I can say is, "Oh."

Miriam continues. "I didn't expect that we would move so soon, but Simon thinks it's best for us. It's beautiful down there and the people are very friendly. You should see his family's house!"

"It does all sound wonderful." I try to hide my sadness, but all I can think is that I will have to start looking for another place much sooner than I thought and that once again, I will have to say goodbye to someone I love. But today is Miriam's day, I tell myself— a day she's long awaited. And she seems truly happy. I will not put a damper on that if I can help it.

She finishes her whirlwind story and turns serious again. "You're really not going to marry Lou, are you?"

I sigh. "Miriam—"

"That's fine. But I have to tell you this is your last chance. I'm going to introduce him to my new friend Nelly Abramson. She's very attractive and single and I know Lou will like her."

"Good," I say, but I notice a funny feeling in the pit of my stomach.

She pretends to be annoyed with me. That is, until she can't contain her happiness for one more second and bursts out laughing.

I know I am going to miss my friend terribly.

12

⊷═◗ ◖═⊶

The job at the millinery store has been very good for me. I like it and it keeps my mind busy. I've become very close to Mrs. Rosen in the year I have worked for her. I've learned she can be both bossy and kind—like having Tateh and Mamaleh all in one.

One morning, she tells me she needs to talk to me and I have a sinking feeling. "Did I do something wrong?"

"Oh no, Bessie. You can do no wrong. It's me—I am too old to make hats anymore. I'm going to close the store."

This is the last thing I expected to hear. Once I recover from my surprise, I ask if there's anything I can do to change her mind. She smiles, but shakes her head. "It is time for me to stop working, Bessie. I'm moving in with my daughter. It will be good for me not to be alone.

"And *you*, darling Bessie, you'll have no problem finding another job. In fact, I heard that Mr. Green was looking for someone to work in his store and I've already mentioned you to him."

I am stunned. "Mr. Green? Isn't that a paint store? What would I do there? I don't know anything about…"

"You're right, Bessie. The job is one he would normally give a man, but I told him how reliable you are and how quickly you learned my business. He agreed to talk to you as a favor to me. I thanked him but I also told him he would end up thanking me instead."

She waits for what she has said to sink in and then continues. "The other problem is that Mr. Green is a Gentile. His store is open on our Sabbath. I told him that if he hires you, you will not be able to work on Saturdays. Be sure to remind him."

I'm speechless. My best friend is leaving and now I must find a new job and a new place to live, all at the same time. Mrs. Rosen pats me on the shoulder. "Life doesn't stand still, Bessie. You'll find it keeps changing and you have to adapt."

Tateh would have said the very same thing.

I go to meet Mr. Green. He reminds me of Tateh, except that his hair is blond and he has no beard. Though he speaks German to me on the first day, he insists that if I am to work for him I must speak English at all times with the customers. I am once again grateful that Miriam refuses to speak Yiddish at home. As I result, I have learned many English words and she and Lou say my accent is much improved. Where I used to have to think in Yiddish and translate into English, I am beginning to think in English some of the time, but I have never heard such perfect English as Mr. Green speaks.

I mention this to him and he smiles. "That's because I was born in this country. So were my parents. Even my grandparents. My family has been in New York for over a hundred years. English *is* my native language. Though my ancestors were from England and Germany, I've never been to Europe. I actually learned what German I know so I could speak with those customers who don't yet speak English."

I feel silly. It has never occurred to me that there are Europeans who came to America so long ago—I still have much to learn about this country, especially if I want to become a citizen.

Mr. Green's store is bright and cheery. The sun streams onto white walls through two large windows in the front. Cans of paint and varnish are stacked atop one another in different areas of the store, brushes hang neatly on hooks and rolls of wallpaper fill shelves in the back.

I have been here now for almost three months and love learning about paint and examining the lovely patterns and textures of wall coverings. But things are very different from my time at the millinery shop.

I remember once that Mrs. Rosen and I didn't hear the bell when a customer walked in. We were too busy talking. That will never happen here. And, of course, Mr. Green doesn't bring in pastries to share with me as Mrs. Rosen did. Mr. Green is often curt and expects me to work diligently without talking much, but William, his son, who also works at the store, says that is just his way.

My primary job is to mix paint and do whatever Mr. Green asks. At first, I mix the paints all wrong, but William demonstrates several times until I learn.

William has a lot more patience than his father. He talks in a quiet tone to the customers. In contrast, Mr. Green speaks in a loud voice—his laugh booms. After making a large sale, he whistles or hums as he walks through the store.

Mostly men come into the store. They are surprised to see me and they want to talk to a man. I smile and show them where the brushes and wallpaper are or mix the paint while Mr. Green or William advises them. Each day I listen closely and learn more about paint and wallpaper. I know now what's right for a parlor but not right for a bedroom and what's right for a bedroom but not right for a kitchen.

But today, I'm doing what Mr. Green calls "woman's work"—dusting the shelves. I don't get upset when he says that—I remind myself how nice he is. Mrs. Rosen said I would have to remind Mr. Green about the Sabbath, but that is not so. In fact, Mr. Green is often the one who reminds *me* to leave at four on Fridays.

⋘═◉═⋙

Simon and Miriam's wedding promises to be the event of Washington Heights. Miriam has asked me to be her "maid of honor," which means I'm helping to prepare for the ceremony and celebration. I go to the dressmaker, hair salon and catering hall with her and help her understand the subtle differences between colors.

I have learned that from Mr. Green and am beginning to think my work is like that of a clothes designer, except that I'm decorating rooms instead of people. In fact, I think I like decorating rooms better than designing clothes. It's much more interesting.

Though I love Miriam very much, I'm getting impatient with her. Everything must be just so—from the dress to the flowers and centerpieces. She hired a man to build an ornate chuppah under which she and Simon will stand during the ceremony and we drop by his shop every day to inspect his progress and ensure that every detail is according to her instruction.

Every breakfast and dinner conversation turns into talk about the wedding. Lou ignores her and reads his paper, so I am the one who has to listen, though I am not very interested. Work at Mr. Green's has turned into my reprieve. In the mornings, I can't wait to get to the store.

I shouldn't complain—Miriam has been helpful to me and has begun to send her friends to the store. Because they are women, I advise them, and because this brings in more business, I am ready to ask Mr. Green to increase my pay. The men listen to my suggestions, but they still don't look me in the eye.

⋄⊨◉⊨⋄

In July, Americans celebrate a holiday called Independence Day. This year, I understand much more about the history of America, but I feel dread as the holiday approaches—I promised myself I would deliver the pillow to Nathan Dreizen by then. I ask Lou if he will contact the Glubokoye Society for me to find out where Nathan lives and he promises he will, though there is a part of me that hopes Lou doesn't find him.

When Independence Day finally comes, I go with Lou and Miriam and some of their friends to the bank of the East River. We hold sticks called "sparklers" and watch fireworks. The night sky lights up with red, white and blue. People all over wave American flags while others sway back and forth to band music like I've never heard.

I think of how much my brothers would enjoy this spectacle and I miss them. I look around me—Simon stands with his arm around Miriam. Lou is sitting next to his new friend Nelly. Miriam will soon be married. Will Lou be next? I wonder what I will do.

⊷━◉ ◉━⊷

In early August, in Washington Heights' finest synagogue, Miriam Schaffer becomes Miriam Silverstein. I wear a lace dress and clutch her bouquet as she says her vows.

More slender than she was when I came to live with her and Lou, Miriam is even more beautiful to me than the women we saw in *The Delineator*, her favorite magazine. Her gown bellows outward, sweeping down into a ten-foot long train. Her cheeks are rosy—not so much from rouge as from excitement and happiness. Her hair is arranged in the most fashionable Gibson-girl style and I am reminded again of the way her blond curls used to look in the sun when we played at the lake in Glubokoye.

Simon, on the other hand, is his normal self. Even I, as diminutive as I am, can see that his yarmulke hides his balding hairline from view. It doesn't matter, though—the way he looks at her makes up for any and all of his physical flaws.

The wedding over, a sumptuous feast spread in a ballroom of the most grandiose décor greets us. I glance around the room and see Lillian and her husband as they enter. I glower at him. I have so little respect for the man that I refuse to address him as Herr or Mister Bechhofer.

But I am delighted to see her. We talk briefly until Lazar comes around—it is clear he is in a hurry to leave and she excuses herself to go with him. She promises to call me, but I can tell from her eyes that it isn't likely to happen.

I glance over at Lou, who is holding a glass of champagne and talking to Nelly Abramson. He invites her to dance and I watch as they glide across the floor. When the music ends, I look up to see Lou walking toward me alone and my heart skips a beat. He asks me to dance.

The champagne has made Lou more forward than usual. He holds me tightly, intimately, as the music plays. "Bessie, dearest," he says, "I love you. I will always love you. Please marry me."

I am taken aback. In Lou's arms, I feel safe and secure, yet something in me still resists. And then there is Nelly. The music stops just in time and I shake my head. "I can't, Lou. I just can't." I walk away from him straight into two of the yentas from the boat.

"Child, you look so-o-o lovely today—one would never recognize you outside of Green's." They howl with laughter.

"And, between your dress and the appearance of Miriam's wedding gown, we'd have to say it's good that she has married a rich man, although she should have married a German instead of a peddler like Simon Silverstein." I turn and hurry outside before I say something I will regret, but not before I hear one of them calling after me.

"When you and Mr. Schaffer stand under the chuppah, we *do* hope you'll invite us."

⋯◦═◦⋯

Now that it's early September, the days are getting shorter. It's still warm during the day, but the nights are cool.

Though they'd planned to go to New Orleans immediately after the wedding, Miriam and Simon only just left. She would never have admitted it, but I know she refused to leave until I found a new place to live.

I moved to a room in a widow's home a few blocks away from Lou's house. The room is small, but includes a bed with a small nightstand, an armoire and a dresser—all more than I need. Newly painted antique white walls greet me every morning as the sun streams in through a large French window.

Mrs. Weiss treats me with kindness, and most importantly, respect. She lets me come and go as I please. She provides breakfast and dinner, though some nights I still eat dinner with Lou and Nelly.

Mrs. Weiss keeps kosher—and she's German—so these days, I eat a lot of sauerkraut, potatoes and veal. The portions are more like at home in Glubokoye. When I eat with her, I am reminded that Miriam and Lou have been here in America so long that they have forgotten what it is like not to have so much. Then it occurs to me that perhaps the reason they have so much is because they have *not* forgotten.

I can't believe I'm saying this, but I miss Miriam's constant chatter. Mrs. Weiss rarely talks. Last week, she left a paper on my bed announcing a class at the German synagogue she attends on "The Proper Etiquette of a Jew." When I mentioned it to Lou, he explained that the German Jews occasionally give these classes for other Jews to "help" us, that they are embarrassed by Russian Jews because we are mostly poor and they are afraid the Gentiles will lump all Jews together. I wadded up the paper and discarded it at the store.

In just a few weeks, I will be twenty years old. Miriam has begged me to come to New Orleans to celebrate my birthday. She says Simon will pay, but I tell her that I have already taken off too much time from the store.

13

❖━◉⊜━❖

I have waited long enough. I will take the pillow to Nathan Dreizen this week. Last night at dinner, Lou told me what he had learned about him from members of the Glubokoye Society, and I now have his address in New Rochelle. That is good, except that I have no idea where New Rochelle is or how to get there.

The next day I go to the store early and ask William.

"Why do you want to go to New Rochelle?" he asks.

"Oh," I stammer, "I have a friend from Glubokoye who lives there." I don't explain about the pillow—even when I say it in my head, it sounds foolish.

"Well, then," says William, "you'll take the subway and then the train from Grand Central Station. It's on 42nd Street. Trains run every day. My wife has a train schedule—I'll bring it in for you tomorrow."

"Thank you."

William frowns. "Are you going alone? Maybe someone should go with you. Finding the door, much less the right track is difficult now.

The old building is still being repaired because of a terrible accident in the Park Avenue tunnel. Even though the accident was almost five years ago, they're still fixing the tunnel. They're building a new one now that's much bigger. When they finish, it will be wonderful, I'm sure, but right now it's very confusing to get around."

"Oh, I'll be fine. If I'm not sure, I'll ask a policeman." I smile when I say that, remembering that it wasn't so long ago that I was frightened of anyone in a police uniform. I don't even notice them anymore.

True to his word, on Friday, William brings me the train schedule and reminds me to be careful. I'm eager for an adventure and I'm excited. It is only two days away—tomorrow is the Sabbath. On the next day, I'll go to New Rochelle.

I awaken on Sunday and put on my finest green velveteen dress. I inspect myself and decide it's too fancy and replace it with a simpler frock, a plain skirt and a tucked shirtwaist with a bit of embroidery on the collar. I'm not, after all, dressing for an elegant dinner party at Lou's.

When I arrive at Grand Central Station, I find that William is right—it *is* confusing. I scan the area. I see scaffolding and boarded up doors and then I notice a large double-door with people going in and coming out. Once inside, I find myself in a room that is even larger than the Receiving Room at Ellis Island. I am anxious that I will miss the train to New Rochelle, but after a while, I notice a gentleman at a stand with a sign that reads "Information." I purchase my ticket and soon I am on my way.

Once seated on the train, I am calm. It is my first trip out of the city and I enjoy watching as the scenes of the city blend into a bit of countryside. The sun is shining on a beautiful day in America and the future suddenly seems just as bright.

When I depart from the train at New Rochelle, I go into the station and ask for directions. The station manager takes me outside and points me in the direction I must go. He says it is only a short walk.

A few minutes later, I'm standing outside a shed with a rickety wagon next to it. In the field behind, I see two horses grazing. I notice that a large door to the shed is open and I venture in.

"Hello, is anyone here?"

A man in paint-spattered overalls comes around the corner and greets me. "Afternoon, miss. Can I help you?"

"I'm looking for Mr. Nathan Dreizen."

"Well, you're in the right place. He's in the back."

"Yes, thank you, Mr...."

"Excuse me, ma'am. I'm Theodore Wilson, Mr. Dreizen's foreman. Call me Teddy." He grins. "That's what they all call me, even my wife. Unless she wants me to do something for her. Then she calls me 'dear.'" He chuckles at his joke.

I chuckle too. "It's nice to meet you, Teddy. Tell Mr. Dreizen that my name is Bessie Markman and that I'm here with his pillow." The man nods and heads back from whence he came, with a puzzled look on his face.

While I'm waiting, I look around. A bicycle leans against the front wall of the shed, which is cluttered with lumber, buckets of plaster waiting to be mixed, boxes of nails and screws, cans of paint and varnish, rolls of half-used wallpaper. In a corner under an electric bulb hanging from a cord like those in the factory, a small table holds a jumble of papers that look to be invoices and receipts. Beside it are pencils, pens, and a bottle of ink.

I think to myself how Mr. Green would never allow this and then remind myself that Mr. Green is a finicky German—even if he has never been to Germany. And he is certainly not a handsome young Jew, at least not as handsome as the man who suddenly rounds the corner.

I am mesmerized—Nathan Dreizen is tall, taller than Tateh or any men I remember from Glubokoye, with black hair and twinkling brown eyes. Dressed in heavy brown pants, he wears a waistcoat over a white shirt with light blue stripes. The shirt has a tall, stiff collar.

His sleeves are rolled up and I look at his muscular arms. I start to blush and hope he doesn't notice, but he does. He blushes also and rolls his sleeves down.

Before he can even say a word, I introduce myself. "I'm Bessie...*Boshka*...Markman. I'm from Glubokoye. Your mother asked me to..."

"To bring my pillow. Yes, I know. My mother sent a letter and said she'd given it to you at the train station in Vilna. I didn't know how to find you. I assumed the pillow had been lost."

I start to apologize for having kept the pillow for so long and he raises his hand to stop me. He smiles and I see his sparkling teeth. "No matter. You're here now."

I realize that my heart is racing. Our eyes meet and neither of us speaks again until Nathan ventures to break the silence. "Well, Bessie Markman, how do you like New York?"

The next thing I know, I'm telling him about living with Lou and Miriam, about Mrs. Rosen and the millinery shop, about Mrs. Weiss and why I had to move out. I continue, describing my work at "Green's Paints and Wallpaper."

Nathan grins. "You've done well for such a short time in America." He makes a face. "Even if you *are* doing a man's work." I think he may be making fun of me, but for some reason, I'm not annoyed.

He tells me that he buys from stores like Mr. Green's. He hires men to do the painting and wallpaper hanging. He tells me that sometimes his customers need carpentry work and plastering too so he hires various tradesmen as well. He tells me that Teddy Wilson is his loyal, right-hand man and that even though he had to drop out of school in the fourth grade and his English is sometimes dreadful, Teddy can do just about anything with his hands. "He even knows, without measuring, how much paint or wallpaper a room will need. And he's quite a character, as you probably already noticed."

While he's talking, my mind drifts. I wonder if he finds it as curious as I that I work in the same business as he.

He mentions another full-time worker named Ernest and yet another young man who works for him sometimes. His face is animated and his eyes are bright as he tells me his business is growing so much that he hopes he will soon need three or four more. I think he is almost as talkative as Miriam and I am less embarrassed about my own lack of reserve earlier.

He catches himself in mid-sentence and suggests we go outside. I don't see a house and though I would like to know, it would be brazen of me to ask where he lives. I ask what the horses' names are instead.

"Alsace and Glub."

"Alsace and Glub?" I think these are odd names for horses and it shows on my face.

"For Alsace and Glubokoye. It's so I never forget where I came from." He chuckles to himself.

I think to myself that I should have known that. I also think that I like this man who laughs so easily.

Nathan offers to give me a tour of New Rochelle and though secretly I am thrilled at the prospect, I decide it wouldn't be proper to accept such an invitation. I tell him I must return to the city right away.

"Then I'll escort you back to the train station. You can't say no to that." We walk together the short distance back to the station. I have a few minutes before the train arrives, so Nathan sits with me.

"I know who Lou Schaffer is," he says, "but I haven't seen him for a long time. I rarely go to the Glubokoye Society anymore." I tell Nathan about Nelly and explain that now I only see Lou when I dine with them.

The train arrives at the station and I board. When I find a seat and look out the window, I see that Nathan has disappeared and I am oddly disappointed.

14

On Tuesday, I hear the bell ring at the shop and look up to find Nathan standing in the doorway. When I acknowledge him, he walks over to the counter and launches into a speech I suspect he has practiced all the way from New Rochelle. "I can't pretend that I'm here to buy paint, Bessie. I wanted to see you again."

I can't speak.

"Bessie!" Mr. Green's voice bellows from the back room, where he's working on the books. He rounds the corner to see Nathan and changes his tone. "Oh, hello, sir! Can I help you with something?"

Nathan thanks him but shakes his head. "This young lady has been helping me, sir, and she's been doing an impeccable job."

Mr. Green nods. "Very well." He glances at me and then returns to the back room. When he disappears, Nathan leans in.

"Can we meet sometime?"

"Yes, but where?"

"How about a Sunday matinee at Carnegie Hall?"

My heart feels as if a million butterflies are swarming about. I'm not sure what Carnegie Hall is but I've heard of it. "Yes, I would like very much to go with you."

"Sunday afternoon and Carnegie Hall it is. I'll get our tickets this afternoon. We'll hear Nellie Melba. She's the most popular singer in the world. Everyone wants to hear her."

He asks for Mrs. Weiss' address and tells me he'll pick me up there at noon.

"Fine, next Sunday, then," I say in a daze as I write my address on a piece of brown paper on the counter.

At lunchtime, when Mr. Green isn't around, I ask William about Carnegie Hall. He tells me they have concerts and other performances there and that men and women wear their best clothes to go there. He's never heard of Nellie Melba but tells me if it's a performance at Carnegie Hall, it will be splendid.

⟡⟢

On Sunday morning, I wake more excited than on any day since I've been in America. Before noon, I am dressed in one of my prettiest gowns. By the time Nathan arrives in the carriage, I feel like a princess, and by the time we leave Carnegie Hall, I want the day to last forever.

On the carriage ride back to Mrs. Weiss's house, Nathan says, "You are beautiful. And your dress! Certainly Mr. Green doesn't pay such generous wages that you can afford such an elegant frock."

I laugh, not sure if I should be shocked or annoyed. "No, you're right. He doesn't. When I lived with Miriam and Lou Schaffer I was able to put most of my wages away."

After that, Nathan becomes a regular fixture at Mrs. Weiss's. One afternoon, he seems pensive and asks why I came to America alone, without my family. I know that he knows about the pogroms, but I tell him that Tateh and Mamaleh were afraid of what would happen to me and how I wanted a life with opportunity. I tell him about going with Tateh to sell goods to the Russian military.

"Well, now that you've been here a while, what do you think of America?" he asks.

I think for a moment. "America is more complicated than I ever imagined. When I came here, I was a girl. Now I feel like a woman."

I tell him about working at the factory, about Rachael and Ezra. I realize that I've never mentioned any of this to anyone other than Miriam and Lou. I'm amazed at how easy it is to talk with him. "It's not easy, but I'm earning money and paying my room and board, even if it *is* man's work." We both giggle.

I can tell Nathan is touched by my story about Rachael. He tells me that he too was surprised at how many poor Jews live in New York. I tell him about Miriam's wedding, about Lou, and the fact that I'm sure he will propose to Nelly any day now.

He nods his head. "It's the same for me. Everyone I know is getting married. I've been to eight weddings since coming to America."

I feel differently with Nathan than I did with David or Lou. With Nathan, I have butterflies in my stomach every time I'm waiting for him to visit. I worry about silly things like how much to eat or what to wear. Even Mrs. Weiss has noticed.

One evening on the porch, I ask Nathan how he ended up in New Rochelle. He pulls out a cigarette and lights it. "I've never really liked New York, at least the city. I came over from Glubokoye and because of it people think I'm a Russian Jew. At least that's what it says on the form from Ellis Island.

"But I'm not really. Though my mother is there, I was only in Glubokoye for a short time. I was born in Alsace and spent most of my life there. Alsace belonged to France. My ancestors fought with Napoleon. My parents became Germans by nationality in 1870, when Germany took it over, and I guess that makes me German too."

"In any case, I just don't belong in the city. I don't speak much Yiddish, so I don't feel comfortable around the Russian Jews the way you do."

"But Nathan, you like *me* and I'm a Russian Jew."

Nathan takes my hand. "Yes, Bessie I do like you. You are a special woman."

"So, if you're not a Russian Jew, why did your family move to Glubokoye?"

"We lived in Strasbourg. My father, who is no longer living, was a rabbi and a science professor at the Academy of Strasbourg. Life at that time was better for Jews in Alsace than in Eastern Europe. Many Jewish men in Strasbourg became lawyers and doctors, and were generally more comfortable around people who weren't Jewish than those Jews in Russia and the Pale."

I think to myself how ignorant and insulated I am. I didn't know there were Jews in France. And I'd never heard of Alsace.

"Then," he continued, "there was the Dreyfus affair. I think it was in 1895, a Jewish army officer was falsely accused of passing military secrets to the Germans. The repercussion affected all Jews in Alsace—my family fled to Lithuania to escape being killed.

"Eventually all of my brothers and sisters left Glubokoye and came to America. Our name was Von Dreizenstock. A couple of my brothers changed their names to Dreizen when they arrived here, and so did my mother and I.

"My parents had nine children, of which I'm the youngest. My oldest sister had a child before I was even born. I don't see much of my brothers and sisters—they're all much too orthodox for me. I get along okay with my sister Jenny, but my brothers are overbearing—they would have nothing to do with Gentiles if they could arrange it." He pauses. "But don't get me wrong—I'm still observant and I'm proud of our faith and our history."

"I know. You told me that when you first got to New Rochelle, you and your friends had to build a synagogue because there wasn't one. That still doesn't explain why you moved there in the first place."

He thought for a moment. "All of my siblings came to America before me. I came when I was older, with three friends—Ancel Strauss, Ben Bader, and Sam Ulmann. We were all from Alsace originally and remained as close—no, closer than brothers—after our families moved to Glubokoye. We left when it became clear we would not be able to avoid being conscripted by the Russians to fight their war with Japan."

A wistful look appeared on his face. "When we first got here, we wanted to see everything. And we did, but I didn't like much of what I saw on the Lower East Side. The Yiddish theaters were all right, but the filth and poverty in that area of the city, and the lack of aspiration for learning English…it was not for me.

"So, the three of us started taking the Sunday excursion steamers up the Long Island Sound. One Sunday, we stopped at Glen Island Resort. Finding the area beautiful, the next Sunday we skipped the resort and strolled around New Rochelle itself. It's a town with a lot of very rich people who live in mansions. The area was ripe with business opportunities and even if that hadn't been true, you have to admit the town is much more pleasant and easier to get around in than the city."

He shrugged and then smiled, teeth gleaming. "To tell the truth, we moved out here without knowing exactly what we'd do except start a synagogue. And once we were here, I realized all these wealthy people with their country estates needed their homes painted and wall paper hung. So I opened Dreizen's Fine Painting and Wallpapering and started with just one painter, one paper hanger and me."

Nathan looks off into the distance. "It's the best of both worlds, Bess—I can live in New Rochelle, a much nicer place than New York, but I can go there whenever I want to—to go to the museums and the opera, to buy wallpaper and supplies for my customers at Teberg's and now…to see you." I smile and change the subject.

"What is it like to be one of only a few Jews here?"

"It is sometimes hard to keep our traditions in New Rochelle," he says, "but they're important to me and so I do. I keep kosher and attend synagogue on every Sabbath. All three of the men I came with married not long after we moved here and I'm always inviting myself to Shabbos dinner at my friends' homes. Yes, I'm Americanized, but not at the expense of who I am and where I started in life."

I happen to mention that my birthday is coming up soon. His face brightens. "Please, then, let me take you to Glen Island and show you some of New Rochelle." Of course, I agree.

He gives me a gentle hug goodbye and whispers in my ear, "Glen Island, then." More butterflies alight in my stomach.

15

◦⊶◉⊷◦

It is October 3, and I am twenty years old today. Nathan and I board an excursion boat at a pier on the East River. The Long Island Sound glistens in the daytime and it reminds me of the lake in Glubokoye. He tells me that Glen Island isn't so crowded anymore since "The General Slocum" sank, but that the boat we are on is safe. Strangely, with him, I am not afraid.

As we approach, I see a sign that reads: "John Starin's Glen Island Resort: The World's Pleasure Grounds." Chimes atop a Chinese pagoda ring out to announce our arrival.

Eight islands, including those that feature the five cultures of the western world, are linked by causeways and excursion boats. Glen Island includes a beautiful beach, a zoo, even two castles made from stone that were brought all the way from the Rhineland.

We wander through manicured gardens, smile at children riding in miniature wagons pulled by donkeys and laugh at seals performing tricks. Regimental bands march by us and the music is cheerful and lively. We watch as children climb off a steam-driven carousel imported from Antwerp.

Nathan grabs my hand. "Let's ride the carousel." Before I can protest, I'm sitting side-saddle atop a gaily-decorated horse. I hold on tight to the gold pole as the carousel starts up. Nathan sits on another horse beside me.

After riding on the carousel, we settle on a bench and listen as adults and children speaking English, German, Yiddish, and other languages move on and off the boats. They are laughing and smiling— I've never seen anything like it. "Thank you for bringing me here, Nathan. It has been a most perfect birthday."

I hate to leave, but I have to wake up early for work because William will be out. It is my duty to open the store and prepare the register. Mr. Green now trusts me to have a key to the store and handle the money. On the boat back to Manhattan, I steal a glance at Nathan. I'm tiny and people refer to me as pretty, but Nathan is so handsome I think he should be with a girl in a fashion magazine.

When the sun goes down, it is cool on the water. I shiver and Nathan puts his arm around me. It feels good. "Happy Birthday," he whispers.

When we finally arrive at the house, it is obvious that Mrs. Weiss has gone out. As I turn to say goodbye to Nathan in the carriage, he reaches across and takes my face in his hands. His lips touch mine and I kiss him back. Ever so softly and gently he kisses me again, and I tingle all over.

In mid-November, Nathan tells me that we will go to the theater so I can learn more about New Rochelle and buys tickets for a show called "Forty-five Minutes from Broadway." This light-hearted musical pokes fun at people from New Rochelle and makes Nathan laugh out loud. I love the costumes and the music. We walk out singing:

Only forty-five minutes from Broadway / Think of the changes it brings. / For the short time it takes / What a diff'rence it makes / In the ways of the people and things.

I think Mr. Cohan must have written the song for me.

⊷═◉═⊶

At Thanksgiving, Lou and Nelly invite Nathan and me for dinner. I'm disappointed that Yetta isn't there, but as he should have, Lou has given her the holiday off so she can be with her own family. And of course, we miss Miriam and Simon as well.

I have been in America for almost two years now and am thankful for all my friends—especially Nathan. I am sorry I waited so long to deliver the pillow.

During dinner, Lou and Nathan barely speak to each other. Lou asks Nathan a few questions but Nathan says little in response. Nelly wears a small diamond ring. Lou proposed to her in early November and they are to have a small wedding ceremony around the new year. I am happy for them, for him.

In the days leading up to Hanukkah, a collection of dreidels and candles and a second menorah appear in Mrs. Weiss's home. When I question her about them, she tells me that they are gifts for the children at the Hebrew Orphan Asylum. "The settlement house tries to see to it that the children get toys and gifts," she says.

"What is a settlement house?"

"Settlement houses help the poorest immigrants with whatever they might need. My friends and I help out at the Henry Street Settlement House. I'm not a nurse but there's still much to be done and my friends and I do what we can. The people have so little for themselves and their children."

"Would it be all right if I come along?"

"Of course, dear, but as you may know, the conditions on the Lower East Side are dreadful. The orphanage is just one small example. I'm glad that the city finally passed laws to force the landlords of those terrible buildings to make things right. They're mostly Jews, just like us." She hands me a battered old copy of *Scribner's Magazine* opened to an article.

"Here are the pictures Mr. Riis took. These pictures woke people up to the need to make tenement buildings healthier and safer. A group has now hired a photographer to go all over the country taking pictures of children working in factories and mines, so these babies will no longer be forced to work. Just last week, a small boy in Brooklyn lost his arm after his shirt was caught in a machine and there is nothing his parents can do about it.

"We know our work at the orphanage doesn't compare to what others are doing, but it does help in a small way."

I tell Mrs. Weiss about working at the factory and how Rachael died of consumption, and she is surprised. "Bessie, I have underestimated you. You are a remarkable young lady."

I mention our plans to visit the orphanage to Nathan. He asks if he can accompany us and when I tell Mrs. Weiss that he wants to come too, she smiles and suggests that we go without her.

When he arrives that Sunday, we discover that Mrs. Weiss has prepared two baskets for us to take. One contains the Hanukkah gifts and some toys and sweets. The other holds warm latkes wrapped in wax paper and a big jar of applesauce she canned back in the fall.

When Nathan and I open the door to the orphanage, some children rush up to us while others stand back and stare. We sing with the children as we light the menorah and play the dreidel game. Mrs. Weiss made the latkes large and thick, so we cut them in half so everyone receives a piece.

The children speak in heavily-accented English though sometimes Yiddish or German amongst each other. The director tells us the children start learning English as soon as they come to the orphanage. Eventually they'll have to make their own way in America, he says, and speaking only Yiddish or German won't help them.

Before we leave, we give the toys and candy to the director of the orphanage and ask that they be passed out to the children during each day of the celebration.

Before I know it, the end of the year has come and Nathan insists that I come to New Rochelle for the Sabbath. He has a surprise for me, he says. I ask Mr. Green to let me off at noon so I can arrive in New Rochelle before sundown and he consents.

Nathan offers to come down to New York on the train to get me, but I tell him it is silly. He tells me that his friends Ancel and Golda Stein have invited me to stay overnight and that we will ring in the New Year with a Shabbos feast like I've never seen and then walk to synagogue Saturday morning.

I pack a few things and take them with me to work. As soon as I leave Mr. Green's, I hurry to the kosher bakery where I buy a nice challah, a fresh apple cake and iced cookies for the children. With my purchases stuffed in my bag, I head for Grand Central Station, and am soon on the train to New Rochelle. As the train pulls into the station, I see Nathan standing on the platform.

Once we arrive at the Steins, I'm greeted by a host of people. I decide that everyone from the synagogue and their children must be there—one couple looks old enough to be my grandparents.

The Steins aren't as rich as Lou or Lillian but they have a large, comfortable home with a spacious parlor, a large kitchen, and a dining room with the largest table I've ever seen. Golda dresses very nicely but not as lavishly as Miriam and her friends. Like Nathan, Ancel has no other family in New Rochelle, so the Stein children think of Nathan as an uncle.

What delights me most is the way the children cluster around him. He puts a brightly painted wooden box with a crank on the floor and tells one of the children to turn the crank. Now we hear a funny tune called "Pop Goes the Weasel." I jump, as do some of the children, when at the end of the tune, the lid springs open and a comical little man in a red and white polka dot suit jumps up. The children laugh.

Golda pretends to scold Nathan for bringing her children another toy and he just grins and shuts the lid on the little man in the red and white polka dot suit again. When every child has had a chance to turn the crank, Golda calls us to the table, which is set with her best china.

She has prepared chicken soup with dumplings, brisket, pickled herring, carrots stewed with raisins, borscht and challah. And if that isn't enough, at the end of the meal, a chocolate cake is brought out and dessert plates set at each place.

I start to pick up my fork when I notice that no one else is eating. Golda is tapping her fork on the side of a glass. A hush falls over the group—even the children are quiet—and everyone looks at Nathan, who is the only one standing. Reaching into his pocket, he pulls out a small box and then kneels beside my chair. He opens the box and says, "Bessie Markman, will you marry me?"

Inside the box is a silver ring with a tiny diamond in the middle. Tears well up in my eyes and I nod my head. He slips the ring on my finger, and then picks me up and swings me around. I can't stop crying and everyone claps.

Once we devour the cake, all the children scamper to the parlor, roll up the carpets and push them into the corners of the room. Ancel winds up the Victrola and we all dance. As we sway back and forth, Nathan holds me close and whispers, "Happy New Year, my darling Bessie."

16

Nathan wants to get married right away and I agree. Our wedding will be in April—April 12, 1908. Nathan says he wants to learn to dance before our wedding. I tell him I know how to dance and that the dance halls in New York aren't very nice places. I think of what the sausage roll vendor said the day I went to the Lower East Side to return Rachael's sweater.

"Bessie," he says, "I would never think of taking you to such places. We'll find a respectable place to dance here in New Rochelle." He does and I have to admit it is great fun. We learn popular new dances like the Fox Trot and the Hesitation Waltz. Dancing with Nathan, who is tall and graceful, is easy. All I have to do is let him lead the way.

I continue to work at Mr. Green's so I can save money before we get married. I'm thinking of going to high school in the evening like some of the other immigrants in Washington Heights. I'm eager to leave New York now and move to New Rochelle, but while I'm still here, I want to take advantage of all the city has to offer.

Nathan places a great value on education. He has told me that his dream is to become a professor at a university like his father. He wants to go to college and after that get a graduate degree. In his spare time, he's always reading—not just Jewish texts, but literature, history, philosophy.

I know he will be a great professor. It will happen. I'll be a wife, and eventually a mother. Professors don't earn much so I will have to work. This suits me fine.

Nathan doesn't think it fitting and proper for a wife to have a job, but it is more, I think, because he believes as a man that he should be the only provider for his family. Like him, I want a good life, a house and a garden, and plenty for my children, but now that I've worked in the world, I need something more than just staying home.

My family will love Nathan, especially Mamaleh, and I know Max and Jack will look up to him. I still miss my family in Glubokoye, but now I'll have a family all my own in America too.

Part Two
New Rochelle

17

Our wedding is tomorrow at Anshe Sholom. Miriam and Simon took the train from New Orleans and arrived yesterday. Simon borrowed an automobile from a friend and will drive Miriam, Lou, Nelly and me to New Rochelle in the morning.

I will wear an elegantly simple white gown of satin and lace. After I purchased it, I took it directly to the Steins' house—where I will dress before going to the synagogue. Miriam brought her pearl necklace for me to wear—it will be beautiful.

Early the next morning, the five of us crowd into the car and set out for New Rochelle. I am both frightened and giddy.

When I enter the synagogue, I see the Steins and their children and all of Nathan's friends. Miriam cries and Lou smiles solemnly as I walk down the aisle holding deep red roses. As we stand under the chuppah, I glance at Nathan in his navy blue serge suit and waist-coat—and know I have made a good choice for a mate.

I suppress thoughts about how much I wish Tateh and Mamaleh were here and focus on how grateful I am for those who have come. They are all my family now.

The Steins insisted on having the wedding supper at their house. Lou and Nelly provided the food as their wedding present to us. And what a feast it is! Just as on New Years' Eve, the children roll up the carpets, Ancel cranks up the Victrola, and we dance while the children pester Simon to take them for a ride in the automobile.

Miriam and Simon gave us a set of fine china dishes with roses along the edges and a white tablecloth for Shabbos. Lou tried to give me money for a down-payment on a house, but I refused. I told him it isn't his job to take care of me and that he should use the money for Nelly and himself. I won't tell Nathan—he knows that Lou has feelings for me and would be offended. More importantly, Nathan would think that Lou believes him unable to take care of me.

At the end of the day, Simon waits in the automobile to take us to Nathan's apartment. I climb into the car and as Nathan closes the door for me, I suddenly realize that my life has changed. I am a wife— there will be no turning back now.

I wave out the window to all of those wishing us well and feel a tinge of sadness as I say goodbye to the city and all my friends there.

⋅─═◉◉═─⋅

It's been three months since our wedding and Nathan and I have settled into a new apartment at 20 Rose Street in New Rochelle. Though we are renters, we purchased new furniture and Nathan had Teddy hang new wallpaper in the living room.

We have plenty of space—a living room, a small dining room, a kitchen, a bedroom, and a bathroom—but I've told Nathan we need to start looking for a small house if we want to start a family.

I spend my days cooking, cleaning and tidying up. Nathan helps me on the weekends, even though cooking for just the two of us and taking care of a small apartment doesn't fill my days. I grew accustomed to getting up early and going to work, either at the millinery shop or Mr. Green's. Though I enjoy being a housewife, I especially miss my days in the paint store. At night, when Nathan comes home, I watch him put the receipts and invoices in order and enter figures in the ledger and I am vaguely jealous.

Nathan's contracting business is growing. When one job is finished, it seems there is always another beginning. I know he's pleased that the business is doing well, but he doesn't talk to me about it. When he's done with the accounting, he goes over to the bookcase and reaches for a book and smokes and reads until I call him for dinner.

A few times a week, a kosher butcher delivers meat to us. I've heard that a Jewish market may open soon, and two friends from Anshe Sholom have started a small kosher restaurant that's open three days a week. We have Shabbos dinner and walk to Anshe Sholom every Sabbath. Several times we have gone to Temple Israel with friends—a reform congregation, it is the other synagogue in New Rochelle.

Other young couples like us live in the apartment building—some are Jewish, some are Christian. We're all friendly and say "hello" to each other. Sophie Beider is a Russian Jew from Courland like David, and Abigail Schiff comes from a small rural village in Germany.

It's no wonder Abigail moved to America. Just as in Russia, Jews in the countryside of Germany are prohibited from owning land and most work for a pittance on land owned by wealthy Germans. In hope of building better lives for themselves, many move to cities like Hamburg or come to America. Among my friends in New Rochelle, it doesn't seem to make a difference where you're from or what religion you practice.

While our husbands work, we meet at one of our apartments once or twice a week for tea and cookies or cake. We laugh, talk and gossip and I begin to understand why housewives often turn into busybodies. There's little else to entertain us. I listen to the gossip, but I don't spread it around like Sophie and Abigail.

Sometimes we speak Yiddish. This is comforting to me, but I don't tell Nathan. When he hears people speaking Yiddish, he almost always comments that if they refuse to speak English, they should at least speak German, the language of educated people.

The truth is Nathan doesn't understand the common Yiddish spoken by most of the immigrants from Russia and it makes him uncomfortable. The Yiddish spoken in Alsace when he was a little boy was different and his father usually spoke German at home.

I remind him that Tateh, as a rabbi, is one of the most educated men in Glubokoye and that he speaks Yiddish.

"Yes, but your father is Russian," is his reply.

I've noticed too that Nathan tends to avoid people who aren't his friends. Miriam commented when she met him that he was very handsome but terribly "bookish."

My husband is a bundle of contradictions—a "bookish" man who works with his hands, a man some think aloof who loves to play with children. He laughs, smiles, and jokes easily when he's around those he cares about and knows well. He is friendly with strangers on the street, shopkeepers, people with whom he doesn't have to converse beyond a word or two. And now I find that he understands French better than I imagined. Nobody I know here or in New York, and certainly not in Glubokoye, understands a word of French.

There is nothing about Nathan that I would change. Except, perhaps, his smoking. The odor lingers in the house and on our clothes and many have begun to say that cigarettes are bad for one's health. I've spoken to Nathan about it before but there's no use continuing the conversation, especially when something is bothering him. He's always nervous about money—paying rent every month, finding his next client—and I know he feels pressured. His dream of a university education, of becoming a professor, keeps being postponed.

One evening, Nathan pores over the books and I can tell he is frustrated. I ask him about it.

"Something is wrong. I think I charged Mr. Rosenblum twice but the O'Connors not at all. I can't remember if Mr. Rosenblum paid me or not. Did he give me cash instead of writing a check? And I'm not sure how much paint I purchased last month. The numbers don't balance." He closes the book forcefully and reaches for a cigarette.

"Nathan, we'll work it out. I can help you," I say as I pick up the invoices and put them in order of the dates they were written. "I have a plan. You know I'm not very busy. All I do is cook, clean and have tea with Abigail and Sophie. I know you don't want me to get a job in a store like Mr. Green's, but what if I did the accounting for your business? That would help you and give me something useful to do. Besides, you'd have more time to read in the evenings."

At first he is resistant. "Oh, Bess, I don't mean to trouble you with my work. I'll learn to handle it."

I try not to show my excitement. "It's no trouble, Nathan. Doing the accounting will make me happy. Besides, Miriam used to do Lou's books—I know how to do it."

He finally agrees and is, I think, relieved, though he doesn't admit it.

I have handled the finances for our household since we were married. The truth is we're financially stable. I buy food as inexpensively as possible and I don't overspend. I loved going to Macy's in Herald Square but I rarely go into New York anymore. From the money Nathan has given me for housekeeping, I've saved $50 in three months, and I have money in the bank from my time at Green's. Secretly, I've been saving for a house. If Nathan's business continues to grow, we could have the down-payment for a mortgage in two years.

We've accumulated a lot since we moved in. We have a davenport with flowered velvet upholstery, a dark wood coffee table and a blue Queen Anne chair. An entire wall is filled with Nathan's books.

Our dark mahogany dining room table is just big enough for ourselves and two guests. And even though the bedroom is small—not much more than a closet—we managed to put a bed large enough for two and a wardrobe in it.

Nathan would probably stay here forever, but I see the apartment as temporary, a place to live before we get our house. I love the location because everything I need is just a short walk away.

Nathan has read that a Mr. Ford will start producing Model Ts in September and explains that the automobile will allow anyone to drive—not just wealthy people. The Model T, he says, will cost half what a Duryea horseless carriage costs now. "Bess, just think, you could drive everywhere instead of walking or taking the trolley."

I suspect that the reason he wants a Model T is because Ancel Stein is going to order one. He longs to have an automobile and I would like for him to be happy, but even at half the cost, it's still too much money for us. A house will have to come first, especially now.

I am pregnant.

The months fly by, and I feel the baby kicking in my belly. In just a month, the baby will be born. I call the baby "him" because it makes Nathan happy. I'm stirring the soup when Nathan opens the door.

"Did today go well at work?"

"Fine," he mumbles. He seems blue.

"Nathan," I say as I stir the soup, "when the baby is older, perhaps you'll have more time to go to school." He looks out the window and I bite my lower lip. I should not have said "perhaps."

When Glen Island opens for the season, Nathan talks Ancel and Golda into letting us take their children under the pretense of giving them a day to themselves. Though he feels his dream of being a college professor slipping away, Nathan does love children. At the end of the day at the resort, the Stein children tell us they had more fun than they would have with their parents. I don't tell Golda this, of course.

Mid-September is still warm and agreeable, but in the last few weeks, I've rarely left the apartment. It is not fitting for a woman in my condition to go out in public. I was able to get away with it longer than most because I carried the baby low until just a few weeks ago. Mamaleh says this means the baby will be small.

Last Sunday, Nathan took the Stein children to Glen Island again—it will close soon for the winter. I was disappointed that

I couldn't accompany them, but I stayed busy canning peaches and stewing apples. Autumn will arrive soon. It's hard to believe it will be my third in America.

In Glubokoye, it's cold by now. Soon it will be snowing. My mother writes letters more often now that she knows our first child is coming. She tells me that if you carry a child low, it's a boy, and reminds me to drink plenty of milk and to rest and take care of myself.

She and Mrs. Dreizen have become friends and Mrs. Dreizen now writes us too, telling us how she wishes she could be here for the birth of her grandchild and how she prays every day for our family. Through her letters, I know my mother-in-law is a sweet woman, a kind soul. I can't help but wonder where I would be if she hadn't approached me in Vilna that day.

It's one of the last Sundays before we will become parents. Nathan is reading a book and rubbing my swollen ankles. I know that the thought of another mouth to feed has increased the strain he feels, though I try to tell him we are fine. "Are you happy about the baby, Nathan?"

"Of course! It's my dream, our dream. I love him already."

My eyes prick with tears and the baby kicks. "Nathan, put your hand on my stomach—the baby is kicking." When he does, I lean over and kiss him on the cheek.

18

Nathan rarely mentions his dream of becoming a professor any-more. Instead, he spends most of his time playing with the children. As I expected, he is a sweet, gentle and caring father—his love for children is one of the things that most attracted me to him.

Joshua is now four and Elisheva, whom we call "Ellie," is three. Like me, she is small—a little lady with beautiful black curls. Joshua is thin and already tall, like his father. While Nathan is working, I often take them to the park to play with other children. I meet other women about my age who are also watching their children.

Now that we have a family, New Rochelle truly feels like home. At Nathan's insistence, from sundown Friday to Saturday night, we observe the Sabbath with strictness. We are more diligent now about attending services at the synagogue—Nathan wants to preserve our heritage and raise our children to be orthodox.

Nathan lives in constant worry even though I remind him the business is flourishing and that we have more than enough. He had to hire two new workers just this week—Eddie Foy, the famous vaudeville comedian, bought a rambling white house two miles from the center of town, and contracted with Nathan for painting and wallpapering. Mr. Foy and his family go all over the country—the comedy "Eddie Foy and the Seven Little Foys" is a very popular show. Mr. Foy is equally amusing at home as well—he named his house "The Foyer."

Nathan says that he feels as if every dollar he puts in the bank is the last one he'll ever make—although he always has a job or two lined up, he is anxious that business will not continue. I try to reassure him that this is not like the old country where no matter how hard one might work there is always the threat that someone will take it all away.

He complains about problems he sometimes has with his workers, and I remind him that all businesses have troubles and that, for the most part, he's blessed with good, hard-working, honest men. Nathan's an honest and caring boss so most of the men like and respect him.

Yes, it's true that they don't always come to work when they should. Sometimes a worker has too much to drink the night before or his wife may be so ill that she can't take care of the children and he must stay home to care for his family. Still others quit, without notice. Some of the workers who came from New York belonged to trade unions and informed him that they received higher wages in the city.

This affected him. He believes that a generous wage is only fair, knowing how much it costs to raise children. Some of his men have very large families and, loving children as much as he does, Nathan feels responsible for them so he now pays them at union scale.

We divided the living room in our apartment into two rooms so Joshua and Ellie could each have a little bedroom. Even though the idea of buying a house overwhelms him, Nathan knows that we have to move to a house as soon as possible. I try to console him by reminding him that in four years, I've saved over $1,000 for a down payment.

Sometimes I think my husband should be running a toy store instead of painting houses. Nathan loves nothing more than surprising the children with toys when he comes home. The house is filled with wind-up toys, crayons and drawing paper. Both of our children have teddy bears, which are all the rage since President Roosevelt was in office.

Unless we're playing together, I keep Ellie's china doll on the shelf so it won't get broken. We made a rule that Joshua's new Lionel train only comes out when Nathan is home, but that means every evening. The train may be intended for little boys, but Nathan and Ellie love it just as much as Joshua. Perhaps it's the time they spend together more than the train itself.

Sometimes picking up the toys takes me almost as much time as cleaning. "Nathan," I say one evening in exasperation, "I'm not sure the children need new toys all the time."

"Oh, it's good for them. It's how they learn." He points to a new wooden jigsaw puzzle with the English alphabet lying on the floor.

"And what of the jack-in-the-box? How are they learning from *that*?" I pretend to be angry, but I am not convincing.

"Ah, Bess, that teaches them cause and effect." He grins and I laugh out loud, which makes the children laugh too even though they don't know the joke their father has made. I kiss Nathan on the top of his head on my way to the kitchen, remembering the jack-in-the-box he gave to Golda and Ancel's children the night he proposed. All this giving makes Nathan so happy and that makes me happy, but I still don't want our children to expect presents all the time.

When Nathan isn't playing with the children, he's using his new camera to take their pictures. Sometimes the photograph is of just one of them playing with a new toy, other times both of them in the park, and sometimes the children and me together. Once in a while, he surrenders the camera to me so I can take pictures of him with the children too.

19

Joshua and Ellie are ill—so ill that I let them rest in our bed. Both have sore throats, high fever and chills. A red rash covers Joshua's face and Ellie, who is drenched with perspiration, tosses and turns in bed. I spent the whole day putting cold cloths on their heads, singing to them, and trying to feed them a warm broth. Dr. Bache finally came today to examine them. He says it is scarlet fever.

When Nathan comes home, he is concerned. "A lot of my workers have said the same about their children. It's spreading. What about the Murphy children next door?"

"They're sick too."

I follow Nathan into our bedroom. Joshua sleeps peacefully, but Ellie is awake again. "Papa!" She reaches for him.

"Hush, Ellie," he says softly. "Lie back down."

"But, Papa, all better now."

He sits down on the bed and she crawls out from under the covers and onto his lap. He kisses her on the forehead.

"Papa, did you bring me something?"

"Hmmm…" he says, pretending that he is thinking. Ellie squeals with joy and Nathan raises his finger to his lips. "Hush, I'll give it to you but only if we whisper. Joshua is sleeping."

He hands her a paper sack. In it are two little hats for their teddy bears—one has flowers and a pink ribbon, the other a black felt top hat with an elastic band.

I bring Ellie's teddy bear from the living room and tuck it—and her—under the covers. Back in the kitchen, Nathan says, "She's coming around. She'll be playing tomorrow and laughing. She's a strong child."

Nathan is right about Ellie. Two days later, I am sitting on the stoop watching my daughter show her teddy bear a leaf. The neighborhood is eerily quiet, absent of other children. The curtains are drawn in all of the windows of the apartment building across the street. I won't let Ellie leave my side.

Joshua is still lying upstairs—Nathan stayed home from work today to tend to him. We've called Dr. Bache, but it will take him a while to get to us with all the sickness—it seems every child in New Rochelle has scarlet fever.

Finally I see a car round the corner and stop in front of our building. Dr. Bache climbs out and I meet him at the door. "Doctor Bache, Ellie seems fine, but Joshua's fever is very high. He has a terrible red rash and his throat is so sore that he has a hard time swallowing even the thin broth I try to spoon into his mouth. He's been vomiting all day."

When we come into the apartment, Nathan greets us and the doctor heads to the bedroom to examine Joshua. We both pace the living room, picking up toys as a distraction while Ellie sits on the davenport.

After some minutes, Dr. Bache asks to speak to us in the kitchen. "I'm afraid it is a severe case. He is indeed having trouble swallowing. I have an elixir that may work, but it's new and I have only a short supply. I can give you enough for perhaps five days—you'll have to find a druggist to get more."

I start to cry. Nathan is pale. "What if it doesn't work?" he asks with a bravery I can't command.

Dr. Bache slowly shakes his head. "If it doesn't work, there's nothing I can do. I suppose you could take him to the hospital."

As soon as the doctor leaves, Nathan gathers up our son in a blanket and takes him to the hospital. Joshua cries in his delirium. I choke back tears—my wiry little son seldom complains.

Hours pass. Nathan returns with Joshua in his arms. I can see the fright in my husband's eyes. "We must pray," he says.

Once Joshua is returned to our bed, Nathan and I sit at the dining room table and pray every prayer we can remember. We light candles and chant and hold hands…and cry in between.

I am lying on the davenport with Ellie. Nathan is asleep in his chair. I drift off to sleep and awaken suddenly. I tiptoe into the bedroom and look at my son. I know even before I reach his side and I am screaming. Nathan is instantly there, restraining me.

"He isn't breathing! He isn't breathing! My son…" I fall to my knees. "We shouldn't have gone to sleep," I say between sobs. "We shouldn't have gone to sleep."

Nathan whispers, "It's God's will, Bessie."

I hear Nathan speaking, but it doesn't comfort me. "Why? Why is this His will?" I collapse into sobs again.

Neighbors I've only spoken with on the stairs or acknowledged at the park soon arrive with food. Jews and Christians rarely visit one another in our building, but when a child dies, the artificial barriers we construct among us fall away. Friends come from Anshe Sholom to sit shiva. I am grateful for such caring people but wish that Tateh and Mamaleh were here with me.

Despite fear of this new plague spreading, the apartment is more crowded than I've ever seen it—people stand in the living room, the dining room, even out in the hallway. We have more than enough men for the minyan.

During the chanting of the solemn prayers, I even see Mrs. Murphy sitting alone in a corner, softly whispering as her fingers move across small black beads.

Then, without warning, Ellie is back in my arms and she is burning up with fever. It has been only a day since Joshua died, but she now has a rash. Ancel comes to take us to the hospital in his new Model T. I am numb.

As we sit by Ellie's tiny bed in the hospital, I hold one of her hands, repeating over and over in my head, "Please, God, don't take my Ellie. I can't lose them both." Nathan, who is disheveled and unshaven, holds her other hand.

I hear wailing and look around. Other children lie in small beds on the ward and desperate parents, just like us, hover over them.

Daybreak comes, then nightfall, then another day. As dusk descends on the third day, the doctor comes to us, shaking his head. "There is nothing more we can do. Your daughter isn't responding to the medicine." Nathan gives the doctor a slow nod, and without a word, lifts Ellie in his arms and carries her out of the hospital.

When we are home again, I glance in the mirror only to see a gaunt, pale-faced woman staring back at me. I wash up a bit, apply some rouge and gather my hair into a bun. As if I am a machine, I open the wardrobe to find a clean dress to wear. I am powerless to help my daughter, but her last visions of her mother will be a woman with a washed face and a clean dress.

I put her teddy bear under her arm and sing a Yiddish lullaby over and over. Her chest rises and falls and she struggles to breathe. "Ellie, my angel, just be calm," I say. "Let go. Your Joshua is waiting for you." I smooth back her hair. She shivers, yet her forehead burns.

Two hours have passed and now Ellie is quiet. She falls into a deeper sleep and her chest relaxes completely, except for a faint rasp. I know the sound—Mamaleh called it a death rattle.

I call for Nathan and together, in silence, we watch as the movement of our little girl's chest slows and then finally ceases. I instinctively place her teddy bear on top of her and cross her arms around him. No longer struggling, she is peaceful and lovely.

I lean down and kiss her forehead. Like my firstborn before her, my daughter will never open her eyes again.

20

⊷⊜⊷

We go through the motions—I wash dishes, clean the house, cook our meals. We have gone backward in time—Nathan works and comes home and we eat supper. He smokes a cigarette and pulls a book off the shelf, though it often lies unopened in his lap.

I'm heavy again with a baby but we rarely talk about it. The same irrational thoughts plague both of us—we should have never gone to sleep the night Joshua died. I should've gone out to the drug store to buy the elixir and given it to Ellie even before the rash appeared.

We decide to donate the children's toys to the Hebrew orphanage in Brooklyn. One evening, while collecting Ellie's china doll to put it in the basket, I notice the camera is missing from its usual place in the closet. "Nathan, where is your camera?"

"I gave it to one of my men."

"Why?"

"It's bad luck to take pictures of the living. There will be no more pictures in this house."

Mrs. Murphy sits on the front stoop with me and listens as I go on and on about what we should have done. I know she understands how I feel—though her children recovered from this epidemic, she lost her first baby to whooping cough.

"Bessie, you and Mr. Dreizen did everything you possibly could for those children. You were wonderful parents. It was God's will," she says, trying to reassure me. I say nothing but dwell upon the words. I am not reassured.

Miriam calls almost every day from New Orleans. I write to Mamaleh and Tateh, and Nathan and I talk to the rabbi at Anshe Sholom in search of comfort. The three of us recite prayers and then Nathan and I go back home. But nothing helps.

Weeks pass. Then one evening, I am making dinner when Nathan comes into the kitchen and sits down at the table. He calls me over—there is a new expression on his face.

"Bessie," he says, taking my hand, "we must stop grieving. We need to think about the baby to come. I want to feel alive again. When I'm at work and one of the men makes a joke, I don't laugh. I avoid walking by the toy store. I've even thought of leaving New Rochelle, moving somewhere else to get away from the sadness." He takes a drag of the Fatima in his other hand. "Then I see other friends and strangers with their children, healthy and happy, and I want to feel that way again."

"You were a good father. You'll soon be a good father again."

We sit quietly for a moment, and then Nathan goes to the closet and rummages around. He returns to the table with a box. I know what it is, but I am not at all sure I am ready. My eyes well with tears.

He removes the cardboard lid to reveal photos of the children. I can't help but look at them and before I know it, my tears have stopped. Nathan gazes at a picture of Joshua and Ellie standing in front of the toy store, each with a new toy. "I remember that day on Mechanic Street," he says.

Suddenly, I smell something burning. The soup! I rush to the stove but there is nothing I can do. The soup is ruined. "Nathan, is the little kosher restaurant on the corner open tonight?"

"I'll get our coats," he replies. His eyes are glistening with tears, but he is smiling.

⋯═◉═⋯

Glen Island Resort closed four years ago. Though people continued to come for a while after it happened, The General Slocum disaster eventually took its toll.

With our once favorite place now long gone, Nathan and I take long walks around Echo Bay, Mechanic Street and Main Street. Although I still wear black and use a parasol to shade myself, the heaviness in the air has begun to lift somewhat—Nathan and I are at least laughing again. Sometimes he even brings me flowers or sweets.

Even so, I still sometimes find myself in a dark place. But, then, the baby inside me kicks and my hopefulness returns. I know Nathan feels better too because he's started talking again about buying a Model T. "Bess," he says, "if we had an automobile we could drive around and look at the mansions on the waterfront. Wouldn't you like to see the house designed by the architect Stanford White? It's owned by the Iselins, the people who started our bank."

I don't know much about architecture but I've certainly heard of Mr. White. An immoral man who kept company with married women and young girls, he was murdered by one of the women's husbands in front of a crowd at Madison Square Garden the year I came to America. I'd love to see the Iselin's mansion but not because of Mr. White.

Nathan continues. "And we could drive by Castleview. It's a convent now but the Leland family used to live in it. Just think, one family living in a sixty-room house! And we could look at the orchids at Rose Hill Gardens and the Thomas Paine Memorial. I was reading about Thomas Paine last night. Did you know his writing helped start the American Revolution? He was from our town too."

I repeat the words to myself. *Our town.* And I smile to myself. It is true—while we weren't paying attention, New Rochelle has become our town.

A letter from Mamaleh arrived yesterday. She writes that the Russians are demanding larger and larger bribes to keep both Max and Jack out of the military. Tateh has been working harder, but it isn't enough. Max and Jack, who are both old enough to be conscripted, work as much as they can as well. Though I continue to send them money when I can, the bribes are taking almost all they have. What I dreaded is happening—despite valiant efforts, Tateh and Mamaleh and my siblings have become poor Jews.

"Nathan," I say in the midst of one of our afternoon strolls, "I would like to bring Max over. He could come second class—it's less expensive and safer for young men than it was for me. And I'd like to bring Jack over too. Mamaleh and Tateh can't afford the passage. Can we send them the money for it? I want to bring over my two other little brothers Eliyahu and Daniel as well, but they're too young to leave Mamaleh and Tateh. It will be a couple more years before they must get out of Glubokoye."

We sit down on a bench and Nathan takes my hand. "We're doing well, Bessie, but it's a lot of money."

"I have saved enough," I say.

"I know you have, but right now, I'm not sure. I'm working all the time, you'll have the baby soon, and the apartment is so small. Where will Max sleep? I can't bear to put the partition back up to make a tiny bedroom like we did for Joshua and Ellie. Besides, having another adult will add to our expenses even more than the baby."

I can hear from Nathan's tone of voice that there's no point in saying anything more right now. But I won't give up on my brothers. There must be a way.

I am sitting in the rocking chair thinking about the baby. I've decided to have him in the hospital instead of at home—it is the modern thing to do in America. The phone rings and I wander into the hallway. I answer it and hear a familiar voice.

"Bessie, it's Lou. I've just received a letter from an old friend back in Glubokoye. He tells me that the Russians are conscripting younger and younger Jewish men and boys and treating them horribly. They're poorly dressed and poorly armed and they're sending them to the front as shields for their men as before."

"Yes, I hear the same things from my family. The Russians are demanding higher and higher bribes to keep Max and Jack from getting drafted. Mamaleh and Tateh are very worried that Max will be drafted in spite of all the money they've paid." I sigh.

"I want to bring Max over but Nathan isn't sure we can afford it. The train fare to Hamburg is more than it was when I came and so is the cost of the steamship. Max would probably be willing to come in steerage but I couldn't bear it. What if he were to get sick? I don't know what to do—but I know that Tateh and Mamaleh don't have the funds."

Lou hesitates for a second. "That's why I called, Bessie. I'll pay the expense of bringing Max to America."

"Oh, no, Lou. Nathan and I couldn't let you do that."

"Please let me help. All my family is here in America now. So is Nelly's. Let us help you bring Max."

I am tempted, but I don't want to accept any more help from Lou. I know Nathan won't be in favor of it. Then a possible solution occurs to me. "Lou, I can't let you pay for all of it, but what if I paid half from money I've saved? It's the only way Nathan would ever consider it."

"You know I'd gladly pay everything. But if you insist, it's all right with me as long as we get Max here."

I am crying as I hang up the telephone but this time they're tears of joy.

When Nathan gets home from work, I tell him the good news. As I expect, he isn't pleased that Lou is going to pay anything but he knows how much I want Max to come. He agrees I've made a good compromise.

⊹━●○●━⊹

The buzzer rings. I push it to open the door at the street, expecting Mr. Shapiro who delivers our kosher meat. I open our door and step into the hallway. Instead of Mr. Shapiro coming up the stairs, it is a young man, haggard and exhausted, with a bag in each hand. I am afraid. I start to scream but then realize who it is. "Max!"

When he gets to the top of the stairs, I almost drag him into the apartment and push him onto the davenport while I run to the kitchen. I take a loaf of bread out of the bread box and slice it for him and then snatching a knife and a jar of strawberry preserves, I set the plate down on the coffee table.

"While you eat this, I'll heat up some chicken soup. There's a big pot on the stove." In another few minutes, I return to the living room with the soup. The bread and half of the strawberry preserves are gone and Max is sound asleep.

When Nathan comes home and sees a man sprawled on the sofa, he doesn't say anything but I know what he's thinking. Since the letter from Glubokoye that said Max was on his way, we have discussed it. How will four people live in this tiny apartment? How will Max get a job when he doesn't speak English? How will we pay for everything?

I walk out of the living room, leaving Nathan with the newspaper, and begin to set the table for dinner. As I place the last fork down, an idea comes to me. "Nathan?"

He looks up from the newspaper. "Yes?"

"Let's rent a house with three bedrooms. We can use the money I have left over to pay the first month's rent. We can borrow a truck—and one of your workers can drive. Max will help carry things. I know in my condition I can't lift anything, but I can certainly pack."

I can tell by his face that I have finally prevailed.

After dinner, Nathan retreats to the living room. Max and I sit at the table conversing in Yiddish. "I want to know everything."

Max shakes his head. "Boshka, things aren't good. It is much worse now even than when you left." He pauses. "We thought for a while that it might get better, but life is hard even for those of us who once lived comfortably.

"I was working long hours, as Tateh and Jack still do. And all of that goes to bribes. If Jack finds a way to come over, he will be one fewer to worry about. But Eliyahu and Daniel will come of age soon enough and it will start all over again.

"The more money we make, the more the Russians know we make and the more they require in taxes and bribes. The boys do all the chores. Mamaleh cooks and cleans."

I pace around the small dining room. "Then we'll bring everyone over. Lou will help us. We will get Jack out first, then the rest of the family."

Max shakes his head slowly. "Tateh and Mamaleh will never leave Glubokoye, Boshka. You may not have been willing to admit it, Boshka, but you knew that when you left. It's a long journey, and too hard to start over, they say. And Mamaleh is afraid she would never learn to speak English. They will, though, permit the boys to come when they turn twelve. I was able to get them to agree to that, I think."

"They want a better life for all of us, but not for themselves?"

Max nods sadly. "Yes, that's how it is. They think it would be too hard."

I get up from the table to pour a cup of coffee for each of us. Max asks about Lillian and I tell him the truth about what happened. He agrees that I did the right thing in not telling Tateh. "It would break his heart," he says. "That you and Lillian are safe and happy gives him hope. And hope is all he has left."

21

⊷═◉═⊷

Moving day comes. I don't carry anything. Nathan won't let me and I know better anyway. Teddy and Ernest help Max carry all the furniture and everything else we've accumulated down the stairs and into a borrowed truck. The house we've rented is also on Rose Street and Max jokes that they could just carry our belongings there. We all laugh at the thought of the spectacle of three men carrying our davenport down the street.

I check the hall closet to make sure we have packed everything but I can't reach a box on the top shelf. I get a kitchen chair to stand on, and hope that Nathan won't see me. I grasp the box and pull it toward me but it slips out of my hands and falls to the floor. Photographs scatter everywhere. My children, Joshua and Ellie, are all around me and more emotional than usual, I begin to sob.

Max comes back upstairs and helps me gather up the photos and put them back into the box. He looks at the photograph of Joshua and Ellie in front of the toy store.

"These are your children?" he asks in Yiddish. I shake my head and he bends to kiss me on the cheek. "They were beautiful," he says. Closing the box, he carefully places it on top of the others he is carrying and goes back down to the truck.

When we arrive at our new house, I marvel at how large it is compared to our old apartment. Our bedroom has room for both a bassinet and crib. Max will take one of the smaller bedrooms. When the baby is old enough, he'll have the third. And then, when Max has his own place, perhaps another child will take what is Max's room now.

Once Nathan accepted the idea of moving, he had Teddy and Ernest paint all of the bedrooms and hang lovely flowered wallpaper in the living room and dining room. The kitchen is a sunny yellow. The floors in the kitchen and bathroom have been scrubbed until they shine.

Nathan, Max, Teddy and Ernest carry the furniture into the house while I supervise. Max keeps us all laughing with Yiddish jokes—even Nathan understands most and I translate for him when he doesn't.

When almost everything is put away and we can see our new home, I find Nathan standing in the living room and slip my arm around him. "Do you like it?'

He smiles at me and nods. "Yes, Bessie, I like it very much."

He and Max walk into the kitchen and out the door into our new backyard. I look out the window and see the two of them standing together. They are smoking and talking and laughing. I look back around at our new and spacious home and touch my swollen stomach and smile. I think perhaps we will make it after all.

22

⊷⊷⊜⊷⊷

Nathan's fears about Max and the load on our household finances
have been, for the most part, unfounded. Since we moved to the
new house, we rarely see him. He works long hours and is up and gone
before we rise. When Nathan comes home from work, Max goes to
his English classes.

Within a month of his arrival, he had secured a job in a jewelry
factory. He was nervous about his English, but my brother's good na-
ture got him the job anyway. In less than two months, Max has be-
friended everyone. He greets every passerby warmly, both to practice
his English and because he genuinely likes people. My friends say to
me, "That brother of yours is funny," or "Your brother is very kind."

Max announced today that he's moving to Brooklyn—he's found
a higher paying job there. Both Nathan and I feel sad to see him go.
I love having him near me and though he hasn't moved out just yet,
I already miss him. But I keep my sad feelings about him leaving to
myself—Max must take advantage of new opportunities.

As I watch Max's train disappear in the distance, my mind shifts to Jack. We'll get him here next. The rumors of a war in Europe have reached New Rochelle and I have to help keep this brother from becoming cannon fodder for the Russian army too.

⟶◉⟵

I have not heard from Mamaleh since my last letter, but Nathan's mother tells us that, by a miracle of God, Jack boarded the very last ship bound for America. Military vessels now fill the Hamburg port and President Wilson has declared neutrality. There will be no more help from America.

⟶◉⟵

When Jack finally knocks on our door, I open it holding a happy and healthy baby boy in my arms. Abraham, or "Al," as we call him, was born in the hospital on Dec. 6, 1913. He developed an infection even before we brought him home which certainly made me fearful that we would lose him, just like Joshua and Ellie. He recovered, but I have changed my mind about having babies in hospitals. I will never again have a child of mine in one.

Like Max, Jack is a good brother to us. Unlike Max, he's quiet and shy. Nathan's business is thriving, our income is stable and our house easily accommodates one more person, so he has none of the concerns he had with Max. The only thing that concerns *me* is Jack's persistent cough. He tells me it's emphysema and assures me that he is all right.

Within a week of his arrival, he was able to get a job at a bookstore in the center of New Rochelle. He taught himself enough English back in Glubokoye that he has been able to move forward quickly. He insists on giving half of his salary to us despite our protests. "For Al," he says. He's asked us also if he can continue to live with us until he saves enough to open a store of his own. He seems to have a good head for business—he notices everything and has observed at the store that the people of New Rochelle often purchase beautifully decorated note cards, envelopes and ornate writing papers. "Everyone writes to their relatives in Europe," he explains.

⋅⊱═◉ ◉═⊰⋅

Time marches on.

It has taken Jack longer than he'd hoped to get the stationery store off the ground, but as with all of my family, he is not afraid of hard work, and the shop is now prospering. On any given Sunday, parishioners of the Catholic Church down the street can be found picking up their Sunday newspapers in Jack's store after the 10:00 Mass. The ladies buy postcards and look forward to seeing the new stationery designs.

Then, one Sunday, with no warning, Jack's regular customers from the church don't come in. When on the following afternoon, Mrs. Flynn, one of his better customers comes into the store, he asks if she knows the reason.

"Because one of our parishioners opened a stationery store not far from here," she says. "Father O'Flaherty told us that we should support our fellow parishioners."

When Jack tells me this, I suggest that he call on Father O'Flaherty and tell him the impact his directive will have on his business, but in his shyness, he refuses. I decide that if he can't do it, I'll have to. I put on a clean dress, nice gloves, and my best hat and walk to the rectory where the priest lives. It's on Center Avenue next to the church.

A pleasant woman opens the door and then disappears to find the priest. When he comes to the door, I extend my hand. "Father O'Flaherty, I'm Bessie Dreizen. My husband's firm painted and hung the wallpaper here in the rectory last spring."

"Oh, yes," says the priest. "Mrs. Dreizen, how may I help you?"

"It's my brother. Until last Sunday, your congregants have been coming to his store to get their newspapers after Sunday Mass. When he asked one of your parishioners about it, she told him that you told your congregation to shop at the new stationery store.

"I'd like to ask you to reconsider, at least with respect to Jack. You see, he came from Lithuania and doesn't have much money. He isn't well and isn't able to do heavy work. My husband and I are very anxious for him to succeed. Is there any way you could help him?"

The priest thought for a moment. "Well, I do appreciate your brother's situation, but I think it my duty to support my parishioners in any way I can." He paused again and then his face brightened.

"Mrs. Dreizen, I see no reason I can't tell them to shop at both stationery stores."

I extend my hand to shake his. "Thank you, Father. You are a kind and compassionate man." I reach in my purse and hand him an envelope. "Please accept this donation for your church."

Father O'Flaherty was as good as his word—on the following Sunday, most of Jack's customers were back.

It occurred to me later that Jack's reticence about approaching the priest wasn't as much about shyness as an assumption that it would do no good. The fears he brought with him from Europe are still fresh. I think about how long it took me to shed my fears of the pogroms and the police. I laugh at the memory of how fearful I was in Battery Park my first day and realize though it took a while, I am no longer afraid.

I've grown to appreciate how special New Rochelle is. Nathan read that the founders came from France two centuries ago to escape similar persecution. They must have understood too.

We received a letter from Max today. He and a friend have found even better opportunities for making jewelry in Attleboro, Massachusetts—a place they say is the "Jewelry Capital of the World." Attleboro is so much further away than Brooklyn that I'll miss him even more than I already do. But, although I know he will not likely come back to New Rochelle, I'm pleased that Max has found his place in America.

23

⟨⋯⟩

Our son Al is growing up fast—he sleeps through the night now. He has dark hair and brown eyes like his father and laughs all the time. I was afraid I would never again be happy after losing Joshua and Ellie but I find myself mostly content these days—I nurse Al, hold him in my arms, rock him to sleep. I pray every night for his health and happiness. I know Nathan is content too. He's even buying toys again.

Yet, in the midst of our happiness, a dark cloud looms in Europe. We've heard the Russians lost a battle to the Germans, who continue to push forward. The news makes everyone here nervous, especially those of us from the old country. The war is not just on the European continent—there are battles in places as far away as South Africa.

I've written to Mamaleh begging her to allow our little brothers to come to us, but she says they want to stay with her. She says now that Max and Jack live in America, though the money they used to bring in is gone, she and Tateh spend less money for food and shelter and pay bribes for only one boy. She says they've even rehired the groundskeeper.

Though she tries to sound bright and cheerful, I sense tension in her writing. I believe the real truth is that she wants to hold onto the last of her children. I've begged and pleaded with her for all of them to come. I've told her that Nathan and I will pay everything and that if I have to go to work myself, I will.

But her answer is always no. I understand—after losing Joshua and Ellie, it will be hard to let go of Al when the day comes that I must. Already, I don't like it for him to be out of my sight for long.

⌖⌖⌖

Our family continues to grow. Chanah was born at home on June 21, 1915. Nathan calls her "Annie." The first time I held my new daughter in my arms, I, of course, thought of Ellie. Ann resembles her—she has the same sweet face, the same hair color and long eyelashes too. When I rock her to sleep, I promise her that I will always protect her.

⌖⌖⌖

Another girl, Florence, is born on December 27, 1916. Her nickname is "Feggy." I make the same promises to her as I did to Ann.

A few months after Feggy's birth, President Wilson finally relented and declared war against Germany. He says it will make the world safe for democracy, but we are not so sure. New Rochelle is now a place of anxiety, especially for those of us who are Russian Jews. The

President has instituted the draft. To those of us from Russia, that is an ominous word.

To try and calm myself, I remind myself that my fears of American policemen were unfounded. Perhaps Mr. Wilson's army will be similar, and won't single out and mistreat Jewish boys as the Russians do. I remind myself constantly that this is not the Pale, but some of the fears I hoped were behind me have risen up again. In times of war—any war—many young men never come home, no matter what their religion or how the officers treat them.

Nathan, because he is responsible for a wife and three children, probably will not be drafted though all men between eighteen and forty-five years of age are required to register. I wept on the day he went to the government building along with other men from Anshe Sholom. He says I am not to worry because during the process the officials asked if he was married and how many are solely dependent on him. He's heard that unmarried men will be drafted first, followed by married men who have no children. I can tell he's more concerned about Max and Jack and his workers than he is for himself. Two of them aren't married, and one who is has no children.

⟶⇒◉◐⇐⟵

Though Nathan is 36 now, the rumors have turned out to be accurate. For the most part, boys of eighteen and nineteen have been sent to battle, including the sons of some of our friends. I breathe a sigh of relief for Nathan, but I still have Max and Jack to worry about.

I haven't heard from Max in a while. Massachusetts is not that far away and yet there is no news.

I mourn when the first of the telegrams arrives. It comes to the mother of one of Nathan's workers. "We are sorry to inform you that your son has been killed in action while bravely fulfilling his duty to his country," it says.

Nathan feels the loss deeply. He always felt fatherly toward Jim, who had worked at the shop in the afternoons and after school from the time he was ten. Jim's father had died, and the oldest of five children, he knew it was his responsibility to help his mother.

Nathan wants to go to the funeral service, but he's nervous because the family isn't Jewish. I volunteer to go with him to the wake. We sit in the back, quietly respectful, but tense. We soon relax as someone stands in front and, though it is not recited in Hebrew, recites a Psalm of David.

The minister of the church seems to be a kind, caring man. He says comforting words to the family that are similar to what our rabbi would say. Despite our differences, we all bury our dead and say prayers for their souls. In silence, I pray for my children, for Nathan, for Jack and Max. I pray for young Colin, Mrs. Murphy's son, who turns eighteen soon. I pray for all the boys on the front lines of this horrible war.

The next day, I sit on our front porch and wait for Jack to come for lunch. Seeing him will lift my spirits, I know. He rounds the corner with a big smile on his face and I stand to give him a hug.

"I'm glad to see you," he says, but before he can say more, he launches into a fit of coughing.

"Jack, I worry about you and Max and this war."

"Don't," he says, when the convulsions stop. "I'm all right. At least I don't have to worry about being conscripted. The army here wouldn't take me because of my emphysema."

While Jack is there, we try to reach Max by telephone. "I'm sorry," says the operator, "but I find no one by that name in Attleboro."

A somber mood descends on both of us.

Yet another contagious illness has arisen. A life-threatening pandemic is infecting thousands both in Europe and here in America. It is a tragic irony but Mrs. Murphy's son Colin had eluded being called to war only to succumb to the Spanish flu.

This flu is so contagious that I am frightened to visit Mrs. Murphy in person. I wept as I talked to her on the telephone. Nathan and I would have attended the funeral, but only the family was encouraged to go. Likewise, though some of our Jewish friends have lost children too, we mourn them privately—no one but close family members sit shiva. In the city, funerals are limited to ten people. Even spitting in public is now against the law and many businesses are shuttered. Nathan's business is affected as well—nobody wants to take a chance of workmen carrying sickness into their homes.

Al is now five years old, Ann is three, and Feggy is two and until this pandemic passes, I will not let my children leave my side, not even to go to the park. Though reports say that the Spanish flu affects mostly young adults, we take every precaution. I make sure they get plenty of rest and give them every elixir I hear is supposed to help. So far, none of our children has developed even a sniffle.

Though the flu continues to take its toll, there is some good news. The Armistice has been signed and the war is over.

⋆⇒◉⇐⋆

It is late in the afternoon, and I hear a knock at the door. A gaunt young man dressed in a "doughboy" uniform is standing on my doorstep. Because of his cap, I cannot see his face.

"Hello," I say. "Can I help you?"

The young man looks up. "Bessie, it's me. Max."

I scream and pull him through the house into the kitchen. The children follow me, curious about this strange man I've invited into our house. I am shaking and drop a loaf of bread on the floor.

I begin to yell at him, tell him how much we've worried, chastise him for not telling Jack and me he'd enlisted. He defends his actions, explaining that he was sent to Europe within a day of his enlistment. "Boshka," he says, "I had no time to say goodbye."

I want to argue that he could have called us but in mid-breath, I realize it isn't worth the energy. All that matters is that my brother is alive and well.

Eliyahu and Daniel remain with my parents in Glubokoye. For a few months during 1917, we were hopeful that things were beginning to change. Sandwiched between the establishment of a provisional government and the October Revolution, many of the longstanding restrictions on Jews were lifted. Mamaleh wrote that some of their neighbors with enough money returned to Moscow and other cities in central Russia from which they'd come. By March of 1918, Russia was no longer involved in World War I.

But peace for the Jews in Russia was not to be—civil war has broken out and my people are once again victims of persecution.

24

❦

We now live in our very own house at 35 Pine Street. I finally convinced Nathan that it was time for us to stop renting and purchase a home. I told him I'd manage the "business end" if he would arrange for all the rooms to be freshly painted and wallpapered. He agreed.

Our new home has a large living room and a separate dining room, a small room we call the "little" room and a kitchen and pantry all on the first floor. Three bedrooms and a bath are on the second floor.

The house has almost all of the new amenities—there is even a basement with its own toilet and a small washroom. When we moved in, there were no electric lights. We thought it would be all right, but after six months of living with gas lamps, Nathan had an electrician wire the entire house.

I'm in the kitchen cooking supper when I hear Al and Annie hollering from the living room. "Mama, you're in the newspaper!"

I assume they're teasing me. "Oh, don't be silly," I say.

Nathan, newspaper in hand, comes into the kitchen with the children on his heels and points at a spot on page 4. "Bess, it's true. Look. Here's your name in the *New Rochelle Pioneer*."

Wiping my hands on my apron, I take the newspaper from Nathan. Under the heading "Mortgages," I see my name.

"Bessie Dreizen to Lena Wellinsky, Oct. 10, 1918, $1,000."

My mouth drops. "Oh my, what will the rabbi say? I'm sure he won't think it proper for a wife to take out a mortgage and then have her name in the newspaper."

Nathan laughs. "I wouldn't worry, Bess. He knows you well enough by now. And besides you're no suffragist. We both agreed that owning a house was a good idea."

An image floats into my mind. *I'm on Fifth Avenue holding a sign. I'm marching with other women side by side.* I laugh and return to my senses. When would I have time to traipse all over the countryside marching in demonstrations, talking to strangers?

The suffragists are the talk of the town. When the Steins and Herschel, the only one of their children still at home, come for dinner one evening, Golda launches into a story about Maude Nathan, a wealthy suffragist from New York. "Bessie, it's scandalous. She's Jewish. She should be home with her children. Just imagine giving speeches everywhere, not just to women but to men too!"

I shrug my shoulders. "Golda, I disagree. Maybe she doesn't have children. The truth is I'm glad some women are working to convince men that we should vote. Of course, I couldn't do what they're doing, but I agree with them. Don't you think we should have a say over our lives?"

Nathan and Ancel are in the parlor discussing automobiles—who's making what, which one is best, how much they cost—when suddenly it is quiet and I know our husbands are listening in. Nathan would never tell me so, but I think he might just agree.

It occurs to me while we're talking how fortunate I am to have lived in Europe and New York and to have seen so much. I love New Rochelle, but I'm sure that having worked at the factory even for a day and to have known people like Rachael and Yetta made me a more caring and compassionate person. I value these qualities in myself.

Despite our differences, Golda has a kind heart and she's a dear friend I don't want to lose, and certainly not over politics. I am in the process of changing the subject of our conversation when Nathan rushes into the room. "Bess," he says. "I've decided to buy a truck."

As soon as the Steins leave, I march into the living room where Nathan is settling in with a book. "A truck! Nathan, we just bought a house. And we're just recovering from the reduction in business because of the flu. Did Ancel talk you into this?"

Nathan is adamant. "A truck will *help* the business."

"Maybe so, but I was hoping we could pay off the mortgage."

"Listen to me, Bess. Many of my customers are quite wealthy. They all have automobiles. It doesn't look right for me to arrive on a bicycle to negotiate a contract. If I have a truck, it will make me look more prosperous, like someone they would wish to do business with."

I consider what he has said and agree. In order for us to be able to pay for both the truck and the mortgage, we decide to rent out the second floor of the house.

Teddy and Ernest divide the "little" room into two smaller bedrooms—one for the girls and one for Al. We turn the living room into two rooms—a bedroom for Nathan and me and another for the davenport, coffee table and Nathan's chair and bookcase. The children will share the upstairs bathroom with renters, and we'll use the toilet and washroom in the basement.

We find renters in no time. A young couple and their baby—the Goldsteins—move in within a month of when Teddy and Ernest complete the project. They are perfect tenants—all we hear from upstairs are footsteps during the day and the crying of a hungry baby at night. We can hardly complain about that—I am pregnant again. We will have our own crying baby again soon.

And, as a result of our decision to rent, we are able to accomplish both of our objectives. I am able to pay down the mortgage each month and Nathan finally has a truck to drive to visit his wealthy clients.

A few weeks later, the children and I come home from an outing in the park to hear loud noises coming from our backyard. Al runs ahead and returns with the news. "Teddy and Ernest are here. They're building a house." Our son is already known for his pranks so I think he is telling me a fib.

"A house? Al, you're teasing me again," I say. But he isn't.

As I round the corner, Teddy hurries over to me. "Afternoon, Mrs. Dreizen," he says, tipping his hat to me. "Mr. Dreizen's havin' me and Ernest build a shed for his new truck. It'll keep out the rain and snow.

"Mr. Dreizen says it's called a *garage*, a French word. Told me that Huguenot Street is French too—named after some French people who started New Rochelle years ago."

He shakes his head in amazement. "And that truck. It's got four cylinders and all. Ain't she a beaut?"

I glance suspiciously over at Ernest, who avoids looking at me while Teddy plows on. "Now this garage, it's big enough for two vehicles, in case Mr. Dreizen decides to buy an automobile."

I try to hide my amusement. It's obvious that my husband has put Teddy and Ernest up to laying the groundwork for yet another purchase.

⊶⊷

The men are back again the next week to hang doors and paint the inside of the garage. Al begs me to let him help. "Mama, Teddy and Ernest might need me. I could hammer. I'm sure they don't have the flu." Al knows I am still careful about exposing my children to any sicknesses, though the threat of illness is much reduced.

"No, darling, I think they can manage. You'll just get in their way."

Teddy grins at Al and then looks at me. "It's all right, ma'am. That youngun won't be no trouble." When I finally consent, he waves Al over. "Come along, son. You just hold this sack of nails while me and Ernest raise these doors up and hammer in the moulding. When I say 'Al, please hand up a nail,' well, then you just dig a nail out of the sack and hand it up. With your help, we'll have her all finished by the time your pa comes home. He can drive that new truck of his right on in this afternoon."

Evening comes, and when Nathan arrives from work, it is just as they say. Al, by now all smiles, shows his father exactly which nails he "handed up," and Nathan responds.

"You did a good job, Al. I'm happy that you helped Teddy and Ernest. I'm sure they appreciated it." Our son beams.

When the inspection is over, the children all beg their father to take them for a ride in the truck and he agrees. I know what that means—with his new truck, Nathan is like a child himself. He will be delighted simply to drive in and out of the garage.

I stay inside while the children run out and climb into the bed of Nathan's new truck. Lying on an old blanket, they look at the stars and make memories that will last a lifetime. I think of all the times I rode home in the wagon with Tateh late in the evenings—there is nothing quite like gazing at the heavens with your father.

We live in a fine neighborhood along with people from all over the world—other Jews, Italians, Germans, Poles. The children and I make friends with all our neighbors, no matter what their religion or what country they're from. All of us are doing well. Our children wear nice clothes and are well fed and everyone is friendly.

Though we are Jewish, Irish Catholics live on either side of us and across the street. Diagonally from our house are the Russos, an Italian family.

The only person in the neighborhood we have any trouble with is Mrs. O'Conner, who lives next door. We are not singled out in any way—Mrs. O'Conner doesn't get along with anybody. If one of the neighborhood children wanders into her yard after a stray ball, she comes out her door with a broom. But, in spite of this crusty exterior, down deep she's a good person. We all know if any one of our children were sick, Mrs. O'Conner would be the first one there with a pot of soup, a loaf of fresh bread and prayers.

I become instant friends with Mrs. Russo and Mrs. Kelly, who lives on the other side of us. It is comforting that we have each other to keep an eye on our children. Best of all, our children get along famously.

One Sunday afternoon, Mrs. Kelly's daughter Grace knocks at our door. "Mrs. Dreizen, Mama said to tell you that Timmy is missing. He disappeared just after we came home from Mass. Have you seen him? He's too little to be out by himself."

"No, dear," I reply, "I haven't seen him but let me ask the children." Before I can even turn around, Al and Annie are out the door to join our neighbors in the search. I am close behind.

After an hour of looking for Timmy without success, I come into the house to call the police. As I hang up, Annie comes running into the house.

"Mama, we found him! He's asleep in the back of Papa's truck."

"Then run over and tell Mrs. Kelly that I'll send Al over with Timmy when he wakes up."

I sit down to catch my breath and smile to myself. Asleep in the back of Nathan's truck. Some things will never change.

⋯⋖══◗◖══⋗⋯

The summer flies by and news comes from Max that he will marry a woman named Helen, whom he met in Attleboro before the war.

The wedding is next week. Nathan has hired a chauffeur-driven limousine to take us to Massachusetts. I think it extravagant but he reminds me that renting the limousine means there will be extra room, so we won't be as crowded during the nine-hour trip.

Nathan clears his throat. "Bess, I've been thinking. Maybe it's time to buy an automobile. Mr. Ford has them coming off the assembly line so fast now they're even less expensive than last year." By now, I know there is little I can say. When Nathan's been "thinking," something usually happens, no matter what I say. Behind closed doors, though, I am troubled.

Golda tells me that Henry Ford has published a set of pamphlets entitled *The International Jew: The World's Problem*. Ancel sold his Model T and drives a Chevrolet now. Other families at Anshe Sholom and most of our Jewish neighbors have chosen to go without an automobile rather than buy a Ford.

Nathan is disappointed, but equally adamant about our need for an automobile. He was fond of saying that Mr. Ford has almost run out of letters in the alphabet, but now I hear more about Durants and Chevrolets.

Still he is pragmatic. "I'm sure all of us buy things from shopkeepers who dislike Jews as much as he does. They just haven't published books."

I am glad that Nathan doesn't worry so much anymore because now I worry enough for all of us. I had grown complacent in the certainty that by coming to America, we had escaped the pogroms, but I'm not so sure anymore.

⊷━◉◉━⊶

Just before Thanksgiving, our son Selig is born and a crib is added to our bedroom. Al is now in the second grade and Annie is in kindergarten. Feggy is not far behind.

Because of the Spanish flu, many parents kept their children home from school. We were among them. I started teaching Al myself—Nathan brought home books, alphabet and number toys, writing paper, pencils and crayons. Ann, so eager to keep up with her brother, insisted on learning right along with him.

Al is friendly and funny, and loves people like his uncle Max whereas Annie is our curious one—she is always asking questions. I say she thinks too much but Nathan disagrees. "She asks a lot of questions because she has a good mind," he says. "So does Feggy. They all do, even Selig. I can tell."

I happen to think he's right.

25

The years have flown by. It's hard to believe we've been married for almost 17 years, yet here it is New Year's Eve, 1924, and I am baking challah and preparing brisket, mashed potatoes, and peas for the extended family. Jack and Sylvie and their two little girls are here and Max and Helen and their children have driven from Attleboro.

Nathan has two helpings of everything. Though he's no longer the slender man I married, I've stopped nagging him about eating too much and smoking too many cigarettes. When I do, it makes him cross and my nagging doesn't change anything.

When I finish the dishes, I come into the living room to find Selig perched on his Uncle Jack's lap. Jack and Sylvie and their two little girls live in Yonkers now. Jack opened a larger stationery store there. I love seeing my brother happy. He sounds so American now—he speaks English so well that he sounds as if he were born here. He loves his work and enjoys talking with customers, though sometimes the talking makes him cough.

I'm glad also that they're still close by so I get to see them. Sylvie is perfect for him. I am so glad that we introduced them—Mamaleh would say that I made a good match.

I sit down beside Jack and we watch our children gleefully playing with their cousins. I think of how proud our parents would be of all of us, and it makes me sad. "I miss Mamaleh and Tateh, and Eliyahu and Daniel," I say. "I wish they'd come here to live."

Jack looks at me sadly and sighs. "I've told you before it won't happen, Bess. Mamaleh's writing again and it sounds like they're doing well again in Glubokoye. We should be happy for that." He sets Selig down on the floor. "We have to count our blessings. For now, we're safe and happy and they're safe and happy."

Lithuania, now a republic, has finally granted Jews autonomy and parity in educational opportunities, even taxation. And this has been another good year for us—the second floor is ours again and Teddy and Ernest have restored the house to the way it was when we bought it. Nathan no longer has to seek out new customers—they come to him. His reputation in the community is well established and it is solid.

Max has done well in the wholesale jewelry business in Attleboro. As usual, he keeps all of us laughing with his stories.

I hear Nathan talking to Max and Helen about the new synagogue in New Rochelle. "Now that the Hebrew Institute has grown so much, they're building a new synagogue on Union Avenue, and I want to be part of it. Ancel tells me it's a congregation with modern orthodox leanings."

I am stunned. I never imagined that Nathan would consider leaving Anshe Sholom. Al is soon to turn 13 and I had assumed his bar mitzvah would be there. I call out to him. "Are you suggesting that we leave Anshe Sholom?"

Nathan nods. "Yes. I know we've always gone to Anshe Sholom but now so many people in our congregation are older. I'm fond of them but they seem stuck in their ways, not modern at all. Many of the younger families have already left Anshe Sholom as you know. If they finish the new building this year, perhaps we can have Al's bar mitzvah there."

Max pretends he is shocked. "Surely Al isn't old enough already for his bar mitzvah. Wasn't it yesterday that he was just a baby?" He grabs my oldest and proceeds to give his hair a good tousling.

"Yes Max," I say, "it's time to start preparing him for his bar mitzvah."

The next thing I hear, Nathan is going on and on about another new gadget he bought. "Come look at my new radio. I caught a couple of the Series games on it."

Al runs to help his father demonstrate how to turn the radio on and I smile at the excitement in Nathan's voice. "The radio is wonderful! I've been listening to President Coolidge on it. It's amazing!

"I'll bet that by New Year's next year, there'll be an announcer counting down as the ball drops in Times Square and Bess and I'll be dancing right here in our living room to the music of one of those new bands."

⇢►●⬤●◄⇠

Today is the first day of February. Though the winter has been unusually cold, Nathan's sister Jenny and Golda Stein and I have been planning a shopping trip to New York for weeks. The children all beg to go with us, but we satisfy them by promising to bring them each a surprise.

We'll go to Macy's, have lunch at Gluckstern's, order ice cream sundaes for dessert, buy chocolates for the children. I hardly remember the last time I was in New York, and I'm looking forward to it. It will be a rare treat indeed.

I go upstairs to my bedroom to change into something warmer, find a clean pair of gloves and my new hat. I ask Nathan to wait until his sister Jenny arrives before he goes out on an errand and he agrees. He is sitting in the dining room talking with Annie about school, and the other children are scattered throughout the house.

Annie calls to me that she's running to the drug store to get something for her father. She asks that we wait until she returns so we can say goodbye. Within seconds, I hear the back door close and then I hear a thump. I assume that Al and Feggy are playing a game and smile to myself.

But the smile is short-lived. I hear Annie scream and the next thing I know, Al is at the foot of the stairs yelling for me. I run down the stairs as quickly as I can and find Nathan lying on the dining room floor. I drop to my knees beside him—his eyes are vacant, his face a bluish-gray. And he's not breathing.

Images of Joshua and Ellie flash through my mind and I start to scream but get control of myself enough to bark orders to Al. "Run as fast as you can to the Kelly's. Tell them we need an ambulance and a doctor immediately." Al hesitates and now I scream in earnest. "NOW! GO NOW!"

Al dashes out of the house and while the girls and Selig stand around their father crying, I put my ear to his chest. I hear nothing.

Within minutes, a siren wails and then I hear the sound of footsteps behind me. On the heels of the ambulance attendants are Mrs. Kelly, with her new baby in her arms, Esther and Moritz Glass—friends from the synagogue who heard the siren—and Jenny and Golda, who pull me away from Nathan.

I watch in shock as the attendants try to revive my husband. It is as if my spirit has left my body as I watch them back away from him and shake their heads. I am surreally calm as, minutes later, I observe Mr. Glass place a candle at Nathan's head, and then the cruel reality washes over me.

My husband is dead of a heart attack at 44. And I am a widow with four children to feed.

26

❖══◯══❖

Nathan lies in a casket. According to our custom, in a sign of respect, his body has not been left alone since he breathed his last. The men from the Hebrew Burial Society washed and dressed him. I don't know who the shomerim were, but Ancel and Jack took care of the arrangements—they moved Nathan's body into the little room and closed the door. Golda remained upstairs with the children until the men finished and said the prayers.

I am seated in my bedroom alone when Jack comes up to sit with me. I can hear his raspy breathing even before he reaches my side. "Teddy asked to be a pall bearer," he says. "But I explained that only Jewish men could perform that task."

I nodded and Jack continued, staring off into space. "'Mr. Markman, sir,' he said, 'I understand what you're sayin' so I guess me and Ernest'll walk behind Mrs. Dreizen and the children, if it's all right with you. Benny could help with the carrying—even though he's only worked for Mr. Dreizen a couple months, he's Jewish. And he's a sturdy lad. You'll need strong men to carry that coffin. Coffins are mighty heavy.'"

I dare not look at my brother. I am sure that if I do, I will crumble into a thousand pieces. "What did you tell him?"

"Of course I told him that we'd be honored to have all three of them. In fact, I told him Benny can take my place. I can't do it because of my emphysema." I nod again—I have always been able to depend on Jack to handle even unpleasant things with grace.

We sit in silence for a while. I study my hands—it is as if they don't belong to me. "Do something for me, Jack. There's a box of photographs on the top shelf in the bedroom closet. I can't bear to look at them. I want you to get rid of them."

He shakes his head. "No, Bess. You should keep the wonderful pictures of the children and Nathan. Especially those."

"You don't understand, Jack. When Joshua and Ellie died, Nathan said it was bad luck to have pictures—that if you keep them in the house someone will die. I should have thrown them out after the children were taken from us. We must get rid of the pictures now or I'm afraid someone else will die."

Jack opens his mouth to argue with me again and then stops himself. He retrieves the box, takes it downstairs and walks to the backyard. I stand at the window and watch as one after the other, the images of my life with Nathan flame and then turn into ash.

❖═◉═❖

I am helping Tateh separate the things he bought in Vilna, placing them in stacks for bundling. "Were you mad at God when Lillian's mother died?" I ask.

"At first. But not for long."

"But you were a rabbi. Why did God let her die so young?"

He stops what he's doing and looks at me with a querulous expression. "That's a big question from such a little girl."

"I was thinking about the pogroms. If Jews are God's chosen people, why does he let bad people hurt us? Did we do something wrong?"

Tateh beckons for me to sit with him and puts his arm around me. "Boshka, God has nothing to do with the bad things that happen to people."

I am frustrated with Tateh's answer. "If God doesn't stop bad things from happening to us, then what good is he?"

Tateh rubs my back. "Without him, we would never be able to pick ourselves up and go on."

❖═◉═❖

Someone tells me to put on my coat. The pallbearers—Max, Ancel, Ben Bader, Sam Ulmann, Abraham "Benny" Wolinsky and Nathan's brother Melvin—carry the casket out of the little room and down the steps to the street. Lou and Nelly stand in the front hallway and Mrs. Murphy next to them—the rest of the faces are a blur.

I can't seem to find my children and then I become aware that Feggy is squeezing my hand. Her little hand is cold. "Run quickly," I hear myself say to her. "Get your mittens. It's freezing outside."

I am aware it is cold for my children's sake, but I feel nothing—not the winter air nor the biting wind. I know I am dressed, and warmly, yet I don't remember changing from my nightgown into clothes. Did Esther help me? I wonder. I know she made sure the children had breakfast. Or was it Golda? Sylvie, perhaps? I think perhaps I am going mad.

Snowflakes fall and melt into the paved streets under our feet as we walk behind the men bearing Nathan's casket. We pass the Boston Spa where Nathan always took the children for ice cream. We pass Ferguson's, Ware's, Beck's Shoe Store, People's Bank for Savings, the Mansion House, City Hall, the toy store where Nathan bought our children gifts. The children stare straight ahead as we walk by. I am holding Feggy's and Selig's hands. On either side of them are Al and Annie.

I see people lining the streets as the funeral procession moves slowly forward. It seems as if all of New Rochelle has come out to pay their respects to Nathan. Some bow their head as the casket passes. Others fall in behind us in the procession—members of the congregation from Anshe Sholom, Mrs. Murphy, our neighbors from Rose Street, our neighbors from Pine Street, our friends from North Avenue, shopkeepers who sold Nathan paint and wallpaper, and all of the men who worked for him. Our lives are passing in front of us.

By the time we reach the Garlick Funeral Home off Main Street, my feet are burning. Jack and Max each take one of my arms and walk in with me. Their wives Sylvie and Helen are close behind with the children.

The next thing I know, we are leaving the service. I know I didn't fall asleep, but I remember none of it.

Nathan is to be buried in the Jewish cemetery in Queens with Joshua and Ellie. Even though he helped to establish the Hebrew cemetery in Greenwich, Connecticut, his brother Melvin insisted that he be buried near our children. I'm happy with that.

Vehicles line up behind the hearse bearing Nathan's coffin. Among them is the truck he was so proud of—Teddy is driving and the men from the shop are piled in the back. Usually a gregarious group, today they are somber. They are fidgety—and tug at the shirts and collars I am sure never see the light of day except for weddings and funerals. Nathan's car is in the caravan too—Ancel and Golda's oldest son is behind the wheel, chauffeuring those like me who do not drive.

We arrive in Queens. After some prayers, I watch as the pallbearers lift Nathan's casket out of the hearse and lower it into the grave. Someone hands me a shovel and I turn it upside down and scoop some dirt. I silently say goodbye to my love and hear the sound—that awful sound of the first dirt as it lands on top of a coffin. And then I hear the chant of the Kaddish and weeping. But I cannot cry.

For the next few weeks, I say very little and wander about the house in a daze. My brothers and their wives, Golda and Ancel, the Baders, the Strausses, the Ulmanns, Mrs. Murphy, and Lou and Nelly take turns making sure someone is with us. Neighbors I barely know bring food.

Miriam, who is pregnant with her second child, calls at least once a week trying to convince me to come to New Orleans and bring the children. It is warmer there, she says. But I can hardly get up in the morning—there is no way I can even think of gathering our things together for a trip. Especially not now.

Esther Kahn comes in the morning and gets the children off to school—I know it is important for them to return to a sense of normalcy as soon as possible, but I have no energy, no will. Without support from my brothers and their wives—and our friends and neighbors—I'm not sure how I will survive.

＊＊＊

A month has passed and on Sunday afternoon, the back door opens. Without having bothered to knock, Nathan's brother Melvin strides in. "Children, leave the room," he commands. "Bessie, I must talk to you." The children look to me with fear in their eyes.

In all the years of our marriage, Nathan and I rarely laid eyes on Melvin. Our children know he is their uncle, but they don't share the closeness and warmth they have with either of my brothers.

I understand why. A few years ago, we accepted an invitation to Melvin's house in Brooklyn for a Passover Seder. It felt like the longest Seder in history—despite their young ages, he demanded my children sit in silence for the entire three hours. He was so stern that they were afraid to move or make a sound, even when he barked at them to recite the four questions. When we left that evening, we thanked him politely and vowed never to have a Seder with him again.

As Nathan told me early on in our courtship, though Melvin was his brother by blood, they were worlds apart in their beliefs and opinions.

I feel heat rise to my throat. I motion to my children to stay and they comply.

"Children, I said to leave this room!" Melvin's voice booms once again.

I raise my voice to match his. "They're eating their lunch and they will continue to do so. Whatever it is you have come to tell me they can hear for themselves. If you traveled this far to tell me something, it must be very important."

Glaring at me, he declares that he has come to take my sons home with him. "I'm their uncle and since my brother is gone, they are now my responsibility," he says. "These boys must be educated like my sons. I will place them in a yeshiva."

Stricken, Al begins to cry. "Mama, no, I don't want to go!" Selig soon joins in.

I stand up and turn to face my brother-in-law. "How dare you walk into Nathan's house and tell me what I should do with our children! They will not go with you—they will not go to a yeshiva. They will attend public school here in New Rochelle and Hebrew school at Anshe Sholom as Nathan and I planned."

"You know nothing. You're only a woman," he says.

Before I can even think, I grab the broom from the corner and swing it wildly at Melvin. "*I* am their mother. *I* will decide what they will and will not do and where they will go to school. Get out of my house! NOW!"

He backs away and through the door, shouting at me all the while. "You're a crazy woman! I'll see to it that the children are taken from you! It's obvious that you're unfit! Mark my words—the state will intervene!"

When they are sure he is gone, Feggy and Selig rush to me in tears. I beckon to Al and Annie to gather around us. "Children, listen to me. Don't ever be afraid. I will always be here with you. Papa is watching over us. No one will *ever* take you away from me."

When I wake the next morning and come down the stairs, the children are dressed and ready for school. Al has helped Selig button his clothes and tie his shoes. Annie has helped Feggy—her hair is combed and a ribbon ties up her hair in the back.

I almost laugh out loud. Through the mercy of God, Melvin Dreizen, of all people, has done what nothing else could do—awaken the will in me. My numbing grief transformed into steel, I suddenly know that I am up to the demands of raising my children alone. They need me. And I certainly need them.

At dinner that evening, we sit around the table talking about the day. Ann is perplexed by something at school. "Mama," she says, "How does everyone know that Papa died? We sang it today in a song."

I raise my eyebrows. "In school you sang a song that says Papa died?"

Al rolls his eyes. "No we didn't."

"*Yes*, we did," says Ann, and she begins to sing. "My country t'is of thee, sweet land of liberty, of thee I sing. Land where my father died…"

Al bursts into laughter. "Ann, the song isn't talking about *our* father. The words are, 'Land where my fathers died…' It's talking about the *founding* fathers. You know, George Washington and Thomas Jefferson. Those men."

"Oh," says Feggy. "I thought it was about Papa too."

At this, Al laughs louder, followed by Annie herself, who finally realizes her mistake. I surprise myself and giggle as well. I glance at

Nathan's empty chair and suddenly know that wherever he is, he is laughing with us too.

In the evening, I climb into bed. The numbness of the past week beginning to lift, I feel an exhaustion set in. I pull the sheets up under my chin and my eyes fall on a tattered but oh-so-familiar object someone has placed on my dressing table. Nathan's pillow.

I retrieve my old friend and snuggle under the covers again, clutching it to my breast. Tears finally emerge from deep within and I sob. I am once again on a journey to a new land alone. And once again, as I did on that train in Vilna, I must place my faith in the promise of Nathan's pillow.

May this pillow bring *us* peace.

Part Three
Going On

27

Spring arrives. The lilac bushes are blooming in the backyard and the bright green grass smells sweet as I stand watching the children start on their 20-minute walk to Trinity School. When we first enrolled Al at Trinity, I questioned Nathan about the school's name. He was well ahead of me—he had looked into it and assured me it was a public school not connected to Trinity Church on Huguenot Street.

It has been three months since he died. I miss him, his handsome face, how he loved the children and me. I miss his books and newspapers, even his cigarettes.

With respect to the contracting work in process, Teddy has been invaluable. I continue to handle the money and pay the men their wages. But it can't go on like this—though Teddy is an excellent foreman, he can't sell. And eventually, all of Nathan's accounts with the vendors will be closed.

For now, Teddy is able to get paint, wallpaper, and materials the men need on credit. He brings me the receipts and I pay the bills. He may not be well educated in the traditional sense, but as Nathan told me the first time I saw him, he has an uncanny eye for how many rolls of wallpaper or gallons of paint will be needed for a job without even measuring. Nathan used to say that he had two choices—one, he could either painstakingly measure everything before bidding on a project or two, just ask Teddy.

Though I'm a woman, I'm the head of the household now. Friends are still helping, but not as often. Lou still comes almost every day to check on me.

I am to meet with Nathan's lawyer, a Mr. Sullivan, this afternoon. He called me earlier in the week to tell me it's important that I come to his office to talk to him. He'll tell me how much money we have left and if all of Nathan's affairs are in order. Lou offered to meet me at the lawyer's office, but I told him not to bother. It's important to me that I handle our business affairs myself.

On the telephone, the attorney spoke frankly. He prepared me for the fact that Nathan had not planned for his death in a financial way. I understand that—he was only 44 and like me, assumed that much of our lives was still ahead of us.

Nathan shared everything with me, so I doubt I will be surprised by anything the lawyer tells me when we meet. I'm fairly sure that Mr. Sullivan will tell me that the only money we have will come from the few jobs outstanding. My thoughts wander to the workers—Teddy has told me that all of the jobs will be complete by the end of the month. When the work stops, their families will suffer too. Like Nathan, I worry about their families. How will they pay their rent?

I distract myself by cleaning and straightening the house. After lunch, I don my spring coat and set out. On the way, I walk past the

Boston Spa and glance at the bonbons and caramels. The ice cream and candy store always reminds me of living with Miriam and Lou and all the fancy shops and restaurants we went to in the early days.

My mind is engaged in "what ifs." Did I fail to see the signs that Nathan was sick? Perhaps he ate too much—he had put on some weight during the years of our marriage. For that matter, so have I. Maybe it was the cigarettes—I certainly nagged him about them, yet at the same time, I've seen men much older than Nathan who've eaten and smoked just as much as he who lived to be nearly 75 years old.

I arrive at Mr. Sullivan's office and hesitate for a moment, taking a deep breath before knocking on the door. A short, red-faced man opens it.

"Mrs. Dreizen, please come in."

I follow him into the room. There are papers everywhere and the office smells of cigars. I remember the day I first saw Nathan and the disarray inside the shed—I can easily see him, in my mind's eye, sitting here, smoking and talking with his lawyer.

Mr. Sullivan motions for me to take a seat and clears his throat.

"I wish I had better news for you, Mrs. Dreizen. The money will run out next month and I mean all of it. Mr. Dreizen made no preparations for you in case of, well, in case of..."

"His death?"

He clears his throat again. "Yes, that's right. Mr. Dreizen was busy building a very good business. He certainly didn't expect this to happen. Of course, you have his truck, his car, his personal effects. You can sell those, but I'm not sure how long the money will last."

I sit back in my chair. "I knew all this, Mr. Sullivan. After all, as you probably know, I kept the books for Nathan's business. I assume everything is in order—thank you for taking such good care of my husband's legal matters."

I start to stand and he holds up his hand. "If you don't mind, I'd like to discuss something with you before you go. I've been thinking about your situation. I've thought about every possible option, and I've come to the conclusion that the only thing that makes sense is for you to take over and run the company."

I feel the blood drain from my face.

He continues. "I know it will be difficult, but Mr. Dreizen himself always said you were at least as skilled—if not more so—than he was in business matters. As you said, you already do the accounting." I can still think of nothing to say.

"The business is solid, Mrs. Dreizen. The workers are good men who will likely want to continue…"

Finally, words come to me. "I couldn't do that. I wouldn't know what to do, how to get new customers. No, I can't imagine…well, perhaps I could…" My voice trails off. Something other than fright about the prospect is emerging.

The door opens and Lou strides into the office. "I'm sorry I'm late. It took much longer to drive here than I expected." Though I am irritated that he ignored my wishes, I am secretly glad to see him.

I introduce the two men and Lou pulls a chair up beside me. When I tell him about Mr. Sullivan's preposterous suggestion, he smiles. "I think that's a perfect idea, Bessie."

He turns to Mr. Sullivan. "You're right. I can attest to the fact that when Mrs. Dreizen worked at Green's, his business more than doubled."

I look at Lou and decide he has gone mad. "But what about the children?"

"Bess, your children are in school all day. Al is a good boy. He can help you. And even though Annie is only nine, like you, she is very capable with numbers. She can help you. And knowing you, the next thing I know you'll learn to drive and you'll get a license."

"But I'm a woman...and a Jew!"

Lou explodes with laughter. "Tell me, Bessie, when did being a woman and a Jew stop you from doing anything? Didn't you come to America alone? Didn't you take the trolley from Washington Heights to the Lower East Side alone? Work at Mr. Green's? Come up to New Rochelle on a train to meet a man without a chaperone, just to return a pillow?"

I can't help but laugh. Maybe they're right—maybe I *can* run Nathan's business.

We sit for moment and then Mr. Sullivan asks Lou to step outside. I can tell he is uncomfortable. "Mrs. Dreizen, there *is* one issue we haven't talked about."

"What is that?"

He hands me a document and I glance at it. I am astounded to see that it is an affidavit declaring my fitness to provide for my children and I understand why Mr. Sullivan is adamant about my taking over Nathan's business. I feel the blood rush to my face.

"What is this? I have to sign that I'm their legal guardian? I'm their mother! Are you telling me that the state is attempting to take my children?" I instantly know who is behind this subterfuge.

"Please stay calm, Mrs. Dreizen. Please. No one will take your children away from you if I can help it. I am *your* lawyer now. As Mr.

Dreizen's wife, you legally own his business, and as I said, I believe the best thing for you—and your children—is for you to take it over and run it. The affidavit simply says you will officially take over the business.

"I know you can do it. Nathan used to talk about how much you know about business and how good you are with the accounting. You have good workers who know what you don't—the truth is that some of them know how to do things that even Nathan didn't. And as for new customers, I know you can't drive, but you do own a car. You can hire a driver to take you about to see customers."

"Say nothing more, Mr. Sullivan." I take the paper and sign on the line next to the X. "I'll keep my children no matter what it takes."

I direct Mr. Sullivan to draw up the additional papers for me to sign so it is official. I will return to sign the new papers the next week.

When I open the door to leave, Lou is waiting for me. He is more serious than before. "Bess, Nelly and I want to give you $1,000 to help with the business."

"Oh, Lou, that's sweet of you, but I don't think we'll need it."

"Neither do I. Think of it as an investment."

We're barely ten feet from the front of Mr. Sullivan's building and I'm already doing calculations in my head. Dreizen's isn't a new business. Nathan always had people pay a third of the cost before he'd start a job. I'll ask them to pay half up front. We already have the tools we need and some inventory and with a little more at the beginning of projects, we'll have plenty of money to buy new paint and wallpaper, pay the workers, and still make a profit.

By the time I reach home, I am even more excited. It's a new world. Women have the vote. And me? I am the owner of a business in New Rochelle, New York.

28

◦─⟦◉⟧─◦

I walk to the school in the morning with the children. Once I've dropped them off, I walk to a house nearby where my men have finished a kitchen renovation—I'll inspect the work with Teddy and do a walk-through with the customers.

The Bells greet me at the door. "How have you been, Mrs. Dreizen?"

I lie. "Fine, thank you."

"Through this way," says Mrs. Bell, who looks at me suspiciously and then points toward the kitchen door.

Teddy is already there puttering about, touching up the paint. The walls are now a sunny yellow. The walnut cabinets have clear glass through which to display the family's finest china. Wainscoting in a small breakfast room off the kitchen contrasts nicely with the small yellow flowers of the wallpaper. A white porcelain sink sits under a window over which a white chintz curtain is draped. Linoleum flooring with black diamonds completes the room. It is lovely and homey.

I turn to the lady of the house. "Are you pleased?"

Mrs. Bell smiles broadly. "Oh yes!"

Mr. Bell ignores me and addresses Teddy instead. "We like it. Fine job."

I study him. I've been in this situation before—Mr. Bell treats me just the same as the men first did in Mr. Green's store in New York. I am invisible.

Teddy says nothing. He may be uneducated, but he is shrewd. He knows, as do I, that what happens in the next few moments could very well determine the success or failure of our new venture together. It's a risk, one that may turn out to be a lapse in judgment, but I must command respect.

Though he towers over me, I step in front of Mr. Bell and slip my hand behind his lapel. "I am the owner of the company, sir, so I would appreciate it if you would address *me* in the future."

He is shocked at what he thinks is my impertinence, but responds appropriately. "Yes, Mrs. Dreizen." I think I see a hint of a smile on his wife's face.

"Thank you." I lead him to a corner of the room. "We will inspect the cabinets, the workmanship, the wallpapering and the paint together. I will make sure it exceeds your expectations. If there are issues of any kind, Teddy will take care of the matter immediately. And when we're done, I will need payment for $342.86, the balance due."

Still speechless, Mr. Bell nods. He starts to question the price and I remind him that we have a signed contract, detailed records of all billings and receipts, and that I am more than proficient in mathematics and accounting.

"I run an honest business, Mr. Bell, and a fair one. I pay my men union scale wages because it's the right thing to do and they have families to support. In return, I expect them to do the best job possible for our customers.

"So far, they've lived up to—no, *exceeded* those expectations and I have no doubt they will continue to do so. As a customer of Dreizen's, you and Mrs. Bell deserve the best. Now, so you and I can get on with the business of the day, we should proceed with our inspection."

I catch Teddy's eye. He and I both know I have no idea of what or how to inspect carpentry or workmanship. Surreptitiously, Teddy stands beside me, pointing out where this paint needs to be touched up, where that corner of wallpaper isn't as tight as it should be. As always, I learn quickly as we go along, but I am most impressed at the beautiful work Teddy and his crew have done. I am proud of the reputation that Nathan had built and will do what I must to carry it on.

"Teddy, you and the others have done an excellent job. Unless Mr. or Mrs. Bell has a concern we've not seen, will you see to it that these few things that need attention are finished by lunch time?"

I look to Mr. Bell and he shakes his head. While I wait for him to write the check for the balance, I talk with Mrs. Bell and hand her my card. "If I can be of further service, please contact me. I noticed that your dining room could use a fresh look, also. I believe you would find the new Japanese grasscloth very stylish."

I stuff the check into my purse and walk quickly from the Bell's to the bakery to buy a lemon cake—the children's favorite.

On the heels of payment of our first new contract, my mind is racing. What if we stopped paying rent and moved the entire shop to

Pine Street behind the house? Teddy and Ernest could easily build a second garage for storage—it would save money and it would be much easier if everything were close by. Things have changed—since I own the house, we don't need a separate place for the shop. And, of course, since we have Nathan's truck, there is no need for horses anymore.

The next morning bright and early, I telephone Teddy to tell him about my new plan. He's enthusiastic and reassures me that building a new garage won't take long. "Could we put in a telephone and running water?"

I think about Teddy's suggestions—a washroom and toilet would be a good idea for the workers. I certainly wouldn't want them in and out of the house all day. And, naturally, we will need a telephone in the shop for when customers call. I decide that we'll wait for the telephone until we've gotten a big job. And I know just where to begin prospecting for new customers.

I telephone my friend Georgia Beckham, who lives in Premium Point with her husband, a banker in the city. I first met Mrs. Beckham at Trinity School—her daughter Dora and Ann are the same age. She knows everyone from the Upper East and West Sides and regales them with the latest news and gossip. When she hears my voice, she invites me over for tea.

I announce myself to the guard at the gate. "I'm here to see Mrs. Beckham."

"Yes, of course, Mrs. Dreizen, go inside. She's expecting you."

I step into the vestibule. The rooms of her home radiate wealth—from Oriental carpets to European statuary to ivory wallpaper with sateen stripes. Mrs. Beckham greets me from the parlor. "Mrs. Dreizen, how good to see you. Let me ring Mary."

We sit down and in minutes, a woman appears with a tea service and a plate of small bites of cake. Mrs. Beckham pours us each a cup of tea and then sits back. "How are you?" she asks. "I mean really—how are you? I've thought of you often since your husband's death."

I sip my tea and take a bite of a petit four. "Well, of course, it's been hard but the children and I are managing. Our friends from the synagogue and our neighbors have been very helpful to us." We talk for a while about our children, the school, community events in New Rochelle and then I reveal why I'm there. "And then, I've taken over Nathan's painting and wallpapering business, so I don't have much time to think about it all. I'm so busy my head spins!"

Mrs. Beckham looks at me with surprise. "I would never have the courage to do such a thing. It does sound very exciting, though."

"The truth is," I replied, "I didn't have time to think about it for long—Nathan's lawyer suggested it and before I knew it, I'd signed the papers."

I set my tea down and dab at my mouth with a linen napkin. "I do hope you'll tell all your friends."

Mrs. Beckham smiles and takes a few of my cards. "I'd be glad to help any way that I can. In fact, I think it would be refreshing to do business with a woman. I mean, most men have so little sense for fashion when it comes to home decor."

Later in the evening, as I'm lying in bed, I reflect on the day. I think of the things Mrs. Beckham and I talked about and feel good about it all. Except for the one untruth I told her. I think about Nathan all the time. I look at the empty half of my bed, pull his pillow close to me and cry myself to sleep.

Next on my agenda is to ensure our continued good standing with Nathan's creditors. Because I paid the bills, I know that he bought most of his paint at Bloom's in New Rochelle and most of his wallpapers from Teberg's in New York.

My visit to Bloom's is less than satisfactory. When I tell Mr. Bloom the situation and ask for his help, he is almost belligerent. "Mrs. Dreizen, I do not offer credit to women, no matter who their husbands are…or were. Good day." Fuming as I leave the store, I remember that Nathan didn't like Mr. Bloom. Now I know why.

As I walk, I remember that, on occasion, there was a receipt from Schwartz's. It is quite a distance away, but by now I am propelled by steam. It is almost closing time when I open the door of the store.

A bell rings and a tiny man with tuft of gray hair and an unruly mustache comes out of the back room. "May I help you, ma'am? We'll be closing in ten minutes."

"I hope so, Mr. Schwartz. I'm Bessie Dreizen, wife of Nathan Dreizen. He passed away—"

"Yes, of course, Mrs. Dreizen. My condolences. Nathan was a good man, one of the best I know."

"Thank you, Mr. Schwartz. I'll be brief. I'm taking over Nathan's business and I ask that you extend credit to me as you did to Nathan and his workers so they could buy paint for jobs. I will pay you in full at the end of each month as we have for years."

He says nothing. His eyes dart around as he mulls this over.

Finally, there is an answer. He smiles and nods his head. "Mrs. Dreizen, I think you are a brave woman. You can buy from me whatever you need."

My hands fly to my heart. Only Teberg's now possibly stands in my way.

I leave the store and it is all I can do not to run all the way home. I'm resolved to do whatever is necessary to bring in the money I must to pay all of our bills and then some. I decide not to bother with contracts except in rare circumstances—there are more than enough honest customers in New Rochelle. Tateh would approve, I know. If I trust them, they'll trust me.

I'll teach Annie—no, she's mature enough now to be called Ann—to prepare and send out the statements. Speaking English hasn't been a problem for me in years, but my writing and spelling continue to be poor. But that is no bother—Ann is more than able to handle that as well.

When I round the corner of our street, I see Nathan's truck in the driveway and Teddy standing outside it with his daughter, Mary, who is crying. My children are crowded around them.

Al and Feggy run to meet me. Not to be outdone, Selig yells, "Annie hit Mary."

"What? Annie, what happened?"

My older daughter, who is red-faced, is standing with her hands on her hips. "Mama, Mary was sitting in Papa's truck where I used to sit. Then she opened the door, jumped out and told me that this is now *her* father's truck and that we can't ride in it anymore."

I look at Teddy, who is obviously embarrassed. "I'm sorry, Mrs. Dreizen. I went by the house on the way to bring the truck back and Mary wanted to ride with me. None of this woulda happened if I hadn't let her. Mary, apologize to Mrs. Dreizen and to Annie."

I look at Mary and shake my head. "It's all right, Teddy. Mary doesn't need to apologize to me. I think the girls have settled this already. However, I do think Ann owes Mary an apology for hitting her. There is no excuse, and I will speak to her later about that. I'll see you in the morning—we need to be at the Heller's around 9:00."

I gather all my children together and head into the house to start dinner. When we reach the steps, I take Annie's hand and talk to her. "You were right, Annie. The truck was your father's. Now it is ours and it will continue to be. Don't be afraid. No one will ever take Papa's truck away from us.

"But you were wrong to hit Mary. I know you were angry, but hurting another person is never the answer." I give her a big hug to let her know I understand how she feels.

I open the back door and step into the kitchen to find yet another surprise. Lou is sitting at my table.

29

I can tell Lou is not himself—if I'm not mistaken, he's even been crying. I motion to the children to go into the other room. "Lou, what are you doing here?"

He looks up. "I came to see *you*, Bess. I'm going to be doing that a lot more often. I'll be here for you and the children now."

I touch his arm. "Lou, I appreciate it, but you can't do that. You have a business to run, and Nelly and Nora and Samuel to care for."

Lou takes my hand. "You've been going through such a hard time that I didn't want to tell you, but the reason I was late to the lawyer's that day was because Nelly took sick. That's why I haven't been around since then."

I look at the bags beneath his eyes and feel the thinness of his fingers around mine. I have a sinking feeling. "Lou, what's going on?"

"Bess, Nelly died three weeks ago. Pneumonia. The doctor said that her body was too weak to fight it off after she went through that bout with the Spanish flu last year. Nothing could be done."

"Oh, my God, Lou," I say, tears streaming down my cheeks. "Why didn't you call me? I would have come immediately."

"I don't know."

I sit down at the table and shake my head. "What did we do, Lou? Why are we being punished?"

After a few minutes, we walk outside together and sit on the front porch. We stare at the horizon until the afternoon sun slips over it and disappears. Here we are again. Lou and me. Family.

Finally, saying nothing, he squeezes my hand, and then goes to his car and leaves.

Another two weeks pass and I come home for lunch on a Monday afternoon to find Lou at my table again. I fix coffee and sandwiches and urge him to eat. He is thinner than I ever remember.

"It's getting warm out," he says.

"Yes, it is," I reply.

It is as if we have been doing this every day for years.

Since that day, Lou has driven up from the city every weekday to have lunch. At first I protested but he would have none of it.

"Bessie, it's easier for me to drive from Washington Heights to New Rochelle than to take the subway to Katz's Deli."

I burst out laughing. "Since when have you ever taken the subway down to the Lower East Side for lunch in the middle of the week?"

"Never," he says. "But I would do it every day if I knew you would be there waiting for me."

⊷⊜⊶

My work schedule is harrowing and I'm often exhausted. Every day is the same—I work all morning, have lunch with Lou, and go back to work until late in the afternoon when I come home to cook dinner for the children. After the children have gone to bed, I record the day's activity and then flop into bed myself.

I've found that running the business isn't just about making decisions about décor. Sometimes solutions require creativity far beyond paint and wallpaper.

One morning, just as the children sit down to breakfast, we hear a commotion in the backyard. Al jumps up from the table to run out and investigate. "Mama, someone is stealing Papa's truck!" he yells.

We all follow him into the backyard and find Teddy peering at something on the ground. "Morning, Mrs. Dreizen, I think we've got a problem." Half of the shop door is lying on the grass.

"What happened?"

"Well ma'am, when me and Ernest and Benny got to the shop, the door was hanging by just one hinge. The wood is rotten—probably from all that snow and rain. Just pulled itself right off the hinge. We figured we'd better go on and take the door down. Didn't want it to fall and hurt a youngun."

"Can't you put it back up?"

"No, ma'am. This door can't be used anymore. And there's not enough wood around here to build a new one."

Teddy knows, like me, that there's not enough money to buy one either, but we can't afford to expose all our tools and paint directly to the weather. I think for a minute and a crazy idea comes to me. "You know those doors in the house between the living room and the dining room?"

"You mean them doors with all the little glass panes?"

"Yes, the French doors. I never shut them—in fact, they're just a nuisance. Why don't you take those doors down and hang them here on the garage? There may not be enough wood to build a whole door, but if they're not quite wide enough, I would think we could come up with enough to fill in either side."

Teddy looks at me and shakes his head. "You know, Mrs. Dreizen, it just might work. We could open them up and still get the ladders out just fine. I'll be in to take a look in a little while."

I turn to go back into the house and smile. Such is the life of Bessie Dreizen these days—and while I wish Nathan were here to share it with me, I love every minute of it.

30

❖══◯══❖

It's 1926. I can hardly believe it, but it's been a whole year since Nathan died.

I observed the traditional mourning period but not as strictly as some might have wished. At Al's request, we postponed his bar mitzvah. We went to no movies or parties and made no special trips to the Boston Spa like we used to.

And, of course, I wore black. But I refused to require my children to. I'm sure Nathan would have heartily agreed. Instead, as I imagine he would have done had it been me who died, I made sure that the children played and laughed and thought of him as much as possible. And I made sure they participated in all the activities at Trinity School.

When I wasn't overseeing projects with Teddy, I was promoting the business. I telephoned and visited all of Nathan's past clients. I attended every business meeting I could, every public meeting. I even joined the newly-established Chamber of Commerce. I ate lunch at women's clubs and made modest donations to philanthropic organizations. And I never left a meeting of any kind without handing out cards and flyers about "Dreizen's Painting and Wallpapering."

But I still held onto Nathan's pillow and cried myself to sleep at night. I still do.

⊷══◉◉══⊶

I'm cooking blintzes for Lou and me today. I mix the dough and roll it out, cut it into squares and stuff some with mashed potato and onion, the rest with fruit and cheese. I hear the door open. "Smells delicious, Bessie. You know I love your cooking."

I look at Lou and realize I've managed to fatten him up a bit. "So that's why you come here!" He smiles and sits down and I hand him a plate with a couple of blintzes and a large dollop of sour cream. He helps himself to a cup of coffee.

"You know, Lou, Nathan's been gone a year, but I still miss him terribly. I have the business and the children have school so we keep busy. But underneath it all, there's still the sadness."

"I know what you mean. I think about Nelly out of the blue and in the strangest places. It happened again just yesterday. I went to dinner at the Algonquin with some business associates. I picked up one of their linen napkins and noticed the monogrammed A.

"Nelly inherited some lovely monogrammed napkins from Mother Abramson, and she loved to use them. I used to pretend that I was offended every time she brought them out. 'But Nelly,' I'd say, 'Schaffer starts with an S, not an A!'" and she'd laugh.

"Of course, I didn't care even a bit. It made her happy. Then, again, last night, Louise set the table with them. I took one look at the

198

napkin and had to leave the table so as not to upset the kids. It took me several minutes to regain my composure."

I slide two more blintzes onto Lou's plate and one onto mine. Funny, but I've noticed that my clothes are getting tighter again too.

As I sit back down at the table, an idea comes to me. "I've been thinking. We should get our children together and do something fun on Sunday. It's been a year since the children had a special day."

"What a good idea! I know…let's go to the Second Avenue Theater on the Lower East Side. We can see Molly Picon in 'Oh, What a Girl!'"

I nod excitedly. "Al and Ann loved 'East and West' when it was here at Loew's. It's such a funny movie—they didn't mind that none of the characters ever spoke a word. Nathan didn't care for it but he loved that Al and Ann had such fun. Now that I think of it, Feggy and Selig have never been to the theater.

"And after the show, let's have an early supper at Ratner's! I've always wanted to go there. The children and I will take the train to Grand Central. Then we'll take a taxi down to the theater and meet you there."

Lou grins. "It's a date, Bess. We'll be waiting for you at the theater door."

On Sunday afternoon, Lou and his children, Nora and Sam, are standing outside the theater when we step out of the cab. Sam is Al's age. Nora is the same age as Feggy. I notice that they both have Lou's dark hair and their mother's blue eyes. And I can see that Lou's business is thriving—the children are beautifully dressed. I'm proud that my four are dressed well also.

Once inside, I sit at one end and Lou on the other, with all of our children between. The music is lively and the story funny, though I admit it is a little less proper than Nathan might have preferred.

Dinner afterward is equally wonderful—the children get along famously and Lou is more animated with them than I've seen in a long time. The truth is that I can't remember when I last laughed so much.

31

"**M**rs. Johnson, I know you're planning on redecorating the whole first floor but let's start with the living room. How would you like to change it?"

"I'd like to start entertaining more, but I'm not sure what to do with it."

I meander around the room, examining the ceiling, the walls, the furniture. I stop at the picture window and look out at her yard, which is mostly wild grass and driftwood. Jagged rocks span the edge of the water. I turn around. "Let me see. We certainly want the room to be lighter, brighter. *And* to reflect inside what you see outside. I think the ceiling should be painted a Parisian blue, with Japanese grass cloth in colors to offset the ceiling's plainness."

I walk around a little more and then point to the waist-high moulding. "To lighten up the room, we can put in wainscoting in a light pine. Those dark rooms of our mothers' time simply aren't in style anymore."

Mrs. Johnson is thrilled with my plan. "That sounds divine, Mrs. Dreizen! When can you begin?"

"I'll need to write an estimate of the cost for you, and once we've agreed, then we can go over the terms of payment. Japanese grass cloth is exquisite but it also very expensive."

"I'm sure my husband will wish to look at the estimate and make the final decision. You know how men are." She pauses for a moment. "The truth is, though, that I'm no good with figures. Can you come back this evening to speak with him? He commutes to New York so it will be around seven when he arrives."

"Certainly." My heart speeds up—if everything goes well, we can start in two days.

The very same week, another new customer contracts with us on my very first visit to tear out her old kitchen and replace everything in it with the newest and nicest amenities. She is delighted with my ideas for the color scheme and furnishings.

I take special care in every home to design in order to match the feel of the room or house. Sometimes I mix the paint myself to ensure the quality and precision of the color—though I had no idea back then, my days at Green's have turned out to be more than useful.

Word of my work trickles out into the community—my attention to the women of the house and the aesthetic possibilities has allowed us to expand beyond what Dreizen's offered when Nathan was alive. Besides, selling to the men is easy. All *I* have to do is please their wives. Things are starting to go very well.

Then, I awaken one morning to find that something is wrong with Feggy. When the doctor comes, he tells me she has rheumatic fever. He reassures me that she will eventually be okay, but will need constant bed rest. I have no idea how we'll get through this.

A few days pass and there is a knock at the back door. It is my brother Max. He puts his arms around me and I begin to cry.

"Bess, it will be hard for you to do what you need to do," he says, "and take care of a sick child. I want to take Feggy back to Attleboro with me for the summer. Helen and I will take care of her."

I am caught between the fear of losing yet another loved one and risking everything we've worked for since Nathan died. But I know Max, and Feggy adores Max, and she loves her cousins too, so I decide to let her go. Max promises to call me on the telephone every day and that he will bring her back the moment she is well.

By the end of the summer, Feggy has regained her full strength. The school year opens and all four of my children—all healthy—march off to school. We note that there are fewer Jewish children at Trinity School this year—many of our friends at the synagogue have moved to nicer homes at the north end of New Rochelle.

In a fleeting moment, I decide we will follow suit. I find a lovely house for sale on North Avenue—a large, elegant house with five bedrooms. At breakfast, I tell the children about it. And then, while I'm putting on my coat, I stop. What will we do with the shop? Where will we mix paint and store supplies? How will the neighbors on North Avenue feel about workers arriving outside their houses in the morning? About the trucks parked on the street?

I think I may have acted impulsively.

I know the children will be disappointed, but I decide we will have to sacrifice some things in order to achieve other more important goals. All my children have high marks in school—and I want them all to go to college. That goal is far more important than their having their own rooms.

The day before our special holidays, the children help me bake yeast cakes for friends, customers and those who are in need, including a few of the war widows who are still struggling. I sit in the cab with the children in the back of the truck as Teddy drives us from house to house to deliver the cakes—I want my children to never forget that life can be hard and we should do all we can to ease the burdens of those less fortunate than we.

My children are all bright like their father—intelligent and talented in their own ways. "Al, Selig," I say, "you boys will be doctors."

"A tooth doctor!" Selig yelps.

"Yes, Selly," I say, as I pat his head. "A *dentist*-doctor."

Feggy has abounding artistic ability but being an artist pays nothing so I push her towards teaching. Ann, on the other hand, has inherited my head for business. She's learning from watching me just as I learned from Tateh. I've noticed that when I meet with the architects, Ann listens in while serving us tea and cookies at the dining room table. I have her keep track of my schedule and I've taught her how to answer the phone in a businesslike manner and write down messages. I remind her to read back the phone number of the caller after she's written it down to make sure she has the right number. Now she reminds me just as often.

She even takes my flyers to local businesses. She's learned just what to say so business owners will agree to put them on their counters or in their windows. And she is not afraid to take the initiative to do whatever must be done.

I don't know what I would do without her. Since I've started meeting with clients in the evening, Ann prepares dinner and oversees the regular household duties. My children are all educated, they are all responsible, they are all kind. Nathan would be proud. I know I am.

My business continues to attract wealthy customers but I often still feel anxious—I will need more customers—perhaps business customers—if I am to pay for my children's educations. It will cost at least $6,000 for each child.

I read in the paper that W. T. Grant is going to build a store in New Rochelle and that those businesses wishing to offer bids for various jobs are asked to make an appointment with the new manager, a Mr. Smithson, within seven days. At first I scold myself for being silly—I have no experience with commercial projects. Then again, I think, I had no experience when I began this adventure either.

I decide I have nothing to lose. I arrange to meet Mr. Smithson, who provides me a listing of the information I need—how many square feet the building will be, the kinds of materials they wish to use, the dates by which they expect to open. I ask questions, listen carefully, and bring home the forms I must submit with our bid.

I talk to Teddy and Ernest. I get their advice on how much paint it will require, how long they think it will take and how many extra men we might have to hire to do the job. I submit our bid and then a week passes, then another. I worry my bid has been too high or that we will be rejected because I am a woman.

Then, one afternoon the telephone rings. "Mrs. Dreizen, this is Mr. Smithson. I'm happy to tell you on behalf of W.T. Grant that you've been awarded the contract to do the painting for the New

Rochelle store. By the way, your work comes highly recommended. How soon can you begin? Some of the walls are ready for plastering."

I try not to act overly excited. "Thank you, Mr. Smithson. I'll speak with my foreman this afternoon and find out when he thinks we can be ready. I will get back to you first thing in the morning."

I hang up and literally run out the back door to the shop. The children, who were crowded around the telephone during my whole conversation, are close behind, whooping and hollering all the way. It isn't long before Teddy and even our shy Ernest have joined us in celebrating.

We agree that I'll tell Mr. Smithson we can start the day after tomorrow. We'll need paint. It will need mixing. We'll need more plaster and more brushes. And more men. There is a lot to do to get ready, but we can do it.

The Grant contract is only the beginning. Because of a recommendation from Mr. Smithson, when the grandson of Elisha Otis, founder of the elevator company, builds a mansion in New Rochelle, we are the company who gets the job of painting and wallpapering.

We are in the midst of the Otis job when I come home one evening to find Dr. Bache's car in front of my house. Suddenly I'm running, screaming.

I run into the living room. Selig is lying on the couch with Dr. Bache bent over him. Ann grabs my hand. "Mama, on the way home from school, Selig could hardly walk. I called Dr. Bache right away."

The doctor stands up and removes his stethoscope. He looks at me with a measure of concern. "It was good that Annie called me right away. I'm afraid Selig has contracted polio. He needs to be in the hospital."

An image of Nathan carrying Ellie flashes through my mind. "No," I say. "He's not going to the hospital. I'll do whatever I have to do, but you will not take him to a hospital."

"But Mrs. Dreizen, he needs constant care. He needs nurses and doctors to attend to him."

I am resolute. "I have you, Dr. Bache. You're my doctor. My children will take care of the house and Teddy and Ernest can run my business for now. Tell me what I have to do."

Seeing that he will not convince me otherwise, the doctor writes down a host of instructions and hands them to me.

In the next few weeks, I follow Dr. Bache's instructions step by step. I sleep in a chair next to Selig every night. And I pray.

This time God hears me.

32

Lou called to say he would miss lunch today but would come later in the afternoon. He is bringing me a surprise, he said.

I am slicing an apple cake when the door opens. I turn to greet my friend and my mouth drops open. Standing in my kitchen is Miriam, with Lou behind her grinning from ear to ear. I remember that she had written to say she was coming for a visit, but in the chaos of Selig's illness and the Otis job, it had completely left my mind.

Miriam hurries across the room and throws her arms around me. "Bessie, I'm so sorry you lost Nathan. I have thought of you every day since I heard. How are you doing? How are you *really* doing?"

I pick up the plate of apple cake and ask Lou to bring the coffee into the dining room. Once we're seated and the coffee is poured, I answer. "The days go by more quickly now. I don't have time to mourn— the children and the business keep me too busy." I cut the cake into slices and pass them around. "Besides," I joke, "apple cake and blintzes make me happy. I've gained twenty pounds since your wedding."

Miriam shakes her head. "And I've gained forty."

We both laugh and then are quiet.

She looks at her brother and then back at me. "It's been a hard year for the two of you."

Lou nods his head. "Yes, it has."

"It's time to focus on the happy."

I nod. "You're right, Miriam. I can't tell you how happy it makes me to see you, to have you here in New Rochelle, even if only for a day or two."

"I'm thrilled to be here with you. You and me, Bess, we'll never change. You're the same girl I knew in Glubokoye. So am I."

We talk about Simon, her children, Simon's business and how much she loves New Orleans. I discuss my children, my business and how I will visit her someday. "Much has changed," she says, "but we'll always be here for each other. *That* will never change."

The next day Miriam takes me to lunch at the Pepperday Inn on Echo Avenue. I've not been to such a fancy restaurant since I lived with Lou and Miriam in New York. I order chilled cucumber soup and trout almandine, while Miriam orders oxtail soup and sirloin tips with roasted red potatoes.

Over Baked Alaska for dessert and coffee served in tiny demitasse cups, Miriam mentions Lou. "I'm so glad you and Lou see a lot of each other. He told me that he has been to see you for lunch every day since Nelly—"

I interrupt her. "Yes, he has. And I have to admit, it's been good to have the company."

"Bessie, you must know Lou still loves you. He always did. I mean, he loved Nelly, but he's always loved you. If you'd marry him, you wouldn't have to traipse around with business cards and flyers all the time. You could relax and enjoy life."

I sigh. "Nothing has changed with me, either, Miriam. Lou is my best friend after you. I need that, but I don't want someone to totally support me—I need to be part of it, I need to contribute in a real way. I don't mind traipsing around with business cards and flyers, as you say—I actually love running the business. Of course I could use the money, the almost instant security Lou could provide, but, as you know by now, I need more than just security."

Before she can ask me another question about Lou, there is a commotion near the entrance to the restaurant. I lower my head and whisper. "Miriam, don't stare but W. C. Fields just walked in the door. Did you know he has a home in New Rochelle? So does Norman Rockwell and Eddie Foy. There are quite a few famous people with homes here on the sound. As a matter of fact, did you know that Nathan and his men painted the Foy home?"

⋅⊱═◉═⊰⋅

I am standing in the kitchen dicing vegetables for a stew.

"Bess, we should make this a new year of fun, of entertainment," Lou says. "We've all been mourning for so long. I'm tired of it. I miss my wife, but I want to move on. Is that wrong?"

"I don't think so. You know I stopped wearing black on the anniversary of Nathan's death."

"Let's move on together. All of us I mean. Let this be a fun year. No war, no disease, no death. Everyone is healthy. It's time to celebrate life again."

210

I throw the vegetables into the pot and turn to face him. "You know what, Lou? You're right. We should go to more movies at Loew's. We can take the children to the Boston Spa. We'll have picnics in Hudson Park."

His face falls. "That's all good, Bess, but that wasn't exactly what I had in mind." I'm pretty sure I know what he means, but I don't respond.

Winter lasts until almost April and then the rains come. During the Easter vacation at school, the children stay inside the house. They are bored and restless. I take Ann to work with me and leave Al in charge of Feggy and Selig.

Finally in May, the dreariness lifts and we begin to spend lazy Sundays at Hudson Park. The children play on the beach. The water sparkles, reminding me of days with Nathan at Glen Island. I try to push away the sadness, knowing that Nathan would want us all to be happy, but it is sometimes harder than it seems.

When mid-May rolls around, the heat comes with it. The temperature reaches the eighties and the beach area at Hudson Park opens for bathing. Lou and I sit on the beach and laugh at the children as they splash in the water.

I brush the sand off my body. My pale face shaded under a large floppy hat, I dare not wear a bathing suit—I've gained at least thirty pounds since I first met Nathan and at 4' 11" inches, I look even heavier than I am.

Every few minutes, a beautiful young girl strolls by and it seems a lifetime since "bathing costumes" were dresses with sleeves and bloomers underneath. I wouldn't dare wear in public the things young women wear today even if I still had the waist of an 18-year-old.

Lou watches Nan and Sam in the water and pays little or no attention to the girls walking by. I study his receding hairline and the fine wrinkles around his eyes.

"We're old," I say.

"What?"

"We're old, Lou."

"Not really, Bess."

"I'm fat. You're starting to get wrinkles."

He feigns horror at the thought.

I laugh. "It's true. You look good for your age, Lou. But I'm fat."

"And more lovely than ever."

A smile creeps onto my face. "Nelly trained you well."

"I'm telling the truth."

I look out toward the ocean and pretend not to hear him.

"Nan is swimming better these days, don't you think?"

33

On Friday, Lou walks into the kitchen and places a gold box with a large purple bow in the center of the table.

"What's this?" I ask, wiping my hands on my apron.

"Open it."

I walk over to the table to carefully untie the bow and peek beneath the tissue paper. Inside is a stylish wide-brimmed white hat with a purple satin ribbon.

"Lou, thank you! This is absolutely gorgeous!"

"Not as beautiful as you."

I touch the ring on my left hand. It has never been anywhere except on my finger since the day of my wedding. "Lou," I say as I look up at him. "I hope you know how much I adore you and your children, but my children are my priority. And over there…," I point to the head of the table, "is where their father—my husband—sat."

He starts to speak and I raise my hand to silence him. "You've always been my best friend. Why can't we just be happy with that?"

He is crestfallen. After a minute of silence, he stands up.

"Whatever you say, Bess," he says, gently squeezing my shoulder as he passes by. "But I'm not going to stop trying."

⊷═◉ ◉═⊷

It's been weeks since Lou's been here for lunch, but as he promised, he still comes once a week to help Al prepare for his bar mitzvah, now scheduled for the fall. I have to say that I am impressed with how well my seldom-serious son is progressing on the prayers and his Torah portion. Al is attending Hebrew school and never misses a Shabbos service.

Sometimes Lou stays and has supper with us. Being with him is easier for me with the children around—our conversations are limited to what's happening at work and in school and other details of our daily lives.

Though Nathan wasn't rigidly orthodox in his thinking, my husband knew more about Judaism and how to read Hebrew than both Lou and I do. It hurts my heart, knowing that my son won't have his father there for this milestone in his life, but Lou's presence has been invaluable.

I thank him for his help. "The rabbi is pleased and says Al will soon be ready for his big day."

"Are you having it at the Hebrew Institute?"

"No, the building isn't finished. I know it sounds crazy but we still belong to Anshe Sholom. Though Nathan was involved with the building of the new synagogue, he was one of the founders of Anshe Sholom and I want Al's bar mitzvah to be there."

I continue to be conflicted over Lou. There's no doubt that I love him but to even look at another man in the way I looked at Nathan feels like a betrayal.

Some of my friends think me unreasonable—that if Nathan could speak, he would tell me his only wish is that I am cared for. I can't talk to Miriam because she is obviously biased and loves Lou too, and I need a friend who can be objective—someone who knows what I've been through, what we've all been through.

And then suddenly, it comes to me. I know just who I will go to.

The August heat and humidity make life unbearable. Thunder booms overhead and rain smacks against my umbrella as I walk to Mrs. Murphy's house for lunch.

My dear old friend ushers me into the living room. "Oh, Bessie, I am so happy to see you. I've missed your smiling face but I know you are so busy with your business. It is very exciting, you know. All the women are envious. I can't imagine how I would manage such a thing!"

We sit at the table and I gaze at my friend. Mrs. Murphy's once flaming red hair is now white but her green eyes still sparkle. "Do you remember my friend Lou? I lived with him and his sister when I first came to America."

"I know Lou came when Joshua and Ellie died. And he and his wife were at Nathan's funeral, of course. But in the confusion and sadness I'm not sure we were ever formally introduced. Wasn't it his sister who married into the Silverstein fortune and moved to New Orleans?"

I nod. "Lou asked me to marry him before I even met Nathan and I said no. Not long before Nathan and I were married, he met and married Nelly Abramson. And then not long after Nathan passed, Nelly died and left him to raise their two children."

Mrs. Murphy gestures for me to go on.

"Until recently, he's driven from Washington Heights nearly every day to eat lunch with me. We've been on outings with all our children, he's brought me gifts, and now he's helping Al prepare for his bar mitzvah.

"It is painfully obvious that Lou wants me to marry him. I'm a widow, he's a widower, and there's no Jewish law against us marrying."

Mrs. Murphy gets up to pour more tea. "I'm afraid I don't understand the problem, Bessie."

"Well," I stammer, "There's no law against us marrying, but I'm not sure I *want* to marry him. Then, the next minute, I'm thinking about him all day. He quit coming for lunch because I hurt his feelings. And that hurt *my* feelings. I loved Nathan so much but..."

"But Nathan is gone, Bessie."

"I know."

Mrs. Murphy smiles kindly. "Then there is only one pertinent question."

"What do you mean?"

"Do you love Lou?"

Without thinking about it, I know the answer.

"Yes."

Mrs. Murphy smiles, her green eyes twinkling. "Then, my dear, I'm not at all sure why we're talking about this."

34

⊷━◉═⊶

The children are back in school. Al is doing well in his bar mitzvah preparations, and Lou comes less and less often now. Since I talked with Mrs. Murphy, I admit it. I *miss* Lou. I miss his teasing, our conversations and laughter at lunch, the way the skin around his eyes wrinkles when he smiles at me, even his receding hairline.

I can't figure out what's going on with me. First I think I love Lou. Then I think I'm being silly. I don't love him like a man I would marry. Well, maybe I do. No, no, of course I don't. What about the children? What about *his* children?

Teddy is driving into New York tomorrow to pick up new wallpaper sample books and rolls of paper for the Heinrich's dining room. I know that Teddy doesn't need me to go with him—we have had an account at Teberg's since when Nathan was alive and they know Teddy better even than me. I decide to have Teddy drop me off at Lou's office in Washington Heights as a surprise. We can have lunch like the old days.

I walk into Lou's office. He is buried behind stacks of paper on his desk and doesn't hear me enter at first. "Hi, Lou. I've come to take you to lunch."

"Bessie! I'm so glad to see you. I'll call my driver right now. And I'll buy instead—we'll go to the Algonquin."

Within minutes, we're on our way to the Algonquin and now I'm wondering if I'm crazy. I have no idea what I'm going to say—I'm not even sure why I'm here. I take a deep breath—everything will be fine as long as I don't start crying.

I order trout almandine with green beans sautéed with tiny onions. Lou orders the same. We eat and talk—about our children, the latest news from Miriam, what I'm doing for the Heinrich's dining room, Al's bar mitzvah. The waiter brings the dessert menu and I choose cherries jubilee. I have no idea what it is but since we're at the Algonquin, I assume it is good. Lou orders sponge cake with chocolate crème. I think of David and *the Moltke* and that night long ago.

Our dessert arrives and it's flaming. I'm startled and Lou starts to laugh. "Why Bessie, I didn't know that you are a liquor drinker. I've never seen you have as much as a glass of wine except at Passover."

"What are you talking about? Of course I don't drink spirits."

Lou gestures at the cherries jubilee. "I hate to tell you, but cherries jubilee has Kirschwasser in it—a flammable liqueur. That's why it burns."

We both laugh and the air around us seems to lighten. We order more coffee and are finishing up our second cups when Lou steals a peek at his pocket watch. I'm running out of time. I must say what I need to say.

"Lou, I don't know what to do. I still love Nathan, but I think I love you too." I start to tear up. "I don't mean to reject you. I just don't know what to do."

He tentatively places his hand on top of mine. "My driver is probably waiting out front. Let's talk about this when we're back at the office."

When we get there, Lou closes the door and takes me in his arms. I bury my face in his shoulder. It is different than with Nathan—Lou is not as tall—but he is just as sturdy.

"We'll figure it out, Bess. One step at a time. How 'bout I drive up for lunch tomorrow? Consider this an order for cherry blintzes."

He grins as we walk to the front door. "But whatever you do, please don't set them on fire."

35

❖═◉═❖

I am recording the day's receipts in my ledger when Selig wanders
into the room, Feggy in tow. "Mama, can we play with all those
tickets on the dining room table when I finish practicing my spelling?"

"What are they for?" asks Feggy.

I lay down my pencil. "They're for a show at Loew's. I met a man
who's an opera singer—Kurt Berger is his name. Two of our workers
are wallpapering his apartment in New York. His wife told me that he
can't get a job, so I rented the theater. If the people of New Rochelle
hear him, maybe he will find a patron here."

Ann overhears us. "Mama, you didn't! What if it turns out like
that silly doctor's book you had us selling all over town? It was awful!
Maybe the reason he can't get a job is that he can't sing!"

"Of course, he can sing. His wife wouldn't have told me he is an
opera star if he couldn't. And yes, I *did* rent out Loew's for his debut.
The manager gave me the whole theater for a good price. After we sell
all the tickets and repay ourselves, we'll give Mr. Berger what's left."

I push away from the desk. "Did I ever tell you that the very first time your father took me on a date, we went to Carnegie Hall to hear Nellie Melba? Her voice was so beautiful."

On Sunday afternoon, the children and I pile into the truck and Teddy drives us around New Rochelle to all our friends' houses to sell tickets to the show. The next week at school, the children sell tickets to their teachers and talk the teachers into buying enough for their friends and families as well.

When the evening of the show arrives, the theater is packed. My children, proud to be part of helping Mr. Berger, are dressed in their best clothes. They smile as people come up to tell us what a fine thing we've done.

The lights dim, the curtain rises, and Mr. Berger begins to sing. He starts with an aria in Italian. The program tells us that it is "Nessun Dorma" from Puccini's newest opera "Turandot."

It is unrecognizable.

He moves on to "Largo al Factotum" from Rossini's "Barber of Seville" and there is rustling in the audience. The children snicker—under his breath, Al starts singing, "Figaro, Figaro, Fe-e-e-garo," and I reach over and poke him with my finger.

Finally, after yet another dreadful aria—this one in French—Mr. Berger announces he'll sing some popular American songs and begins a medley of "Tea for Two," "I'll See You in My Dreams," and "Sweet Georgia Brown." I think it can't get any worse, but it does. When he tries to do a soft-shoe routine, an entire family stands up and leaves.

At intermission, the majority of the audience flows out to the lobby and out the doors into the street. His patron for the evening, we are forced to stay until the very last note.

We invite the Bergers to join us at the Boston Spa for ice cream. While we wait outside the stage door for them, Al tugs at my sleeve. "Mama, how could you have done this? Even Selig knows he was awful!"

Though it is difficult for me not to laugh out loud, I compose myself. There must be a lesson in this somewhere.

"Children," I finally say, "sometimes we succeed and sometimes we fail, but if we don't try we'll always wonder. There's no shame in failing. It's only shameful not to have tried."

It will take quite some time for me to live this one down, but I refuse to stop trying to help those around me.

36

I am late. A week or so ago, when he came to deliver the milk, Mr. Johnson told me that he wanted to buy a house for his family, but that the bank wouldn't make a loan to him unless he had a down-payment. I offered to lend him the money. Like the bank, I told him, I would charge him interest. It would be a win-win situation—they would be able to buy their house and my savings would grow by a small percentage.

The Johnsons are waiting for me when I get to the bank. I withdraw the money from my savings account and give it to them along with the contract I had Mr. Sullivan draw up for us. We all sign it before going inside.

It feels good to help others start out to make a better life. There were those who helped me when I needed it, and it's my turn to help others.

In a matter of minutes, the Johnsons hurriedly leave and the bank president, Mr. Wright, beckons to me to come in. "Mrs. Dreizen, just because you learned how to sign your name doesn't mean that you can give a loan to everyone you know."

"Did you give them a mortgage?"

"No, Mrs. Dreizen. I'm afraid they don't meet the criteria for a loan from this bank."

"Carl Johnson is my milkman. He's wonderful and honest and his wife Betty washes and irons our clothes. They work hard and I trust them. Why shouldn't they live in a house like you and me? They're not a risk for nonpayment. Their mortgage payment would be less than the rent they're paying.

"Give them the mortgage, Mr. Wright. I will co-sign for it. Surely I'm not a risk—if you think so, I suppose I shall take my money elsewhere."

"But Mrs. Dreizen, you have made ten loans within the past six months."

"You're right, I have, and so far, I am making money. I just won the job to paint Mr. Otis's mansion. I've been fortunate. Without the help of others, I would not have been. Now it is my turn to help. I put all of the money I make in your bank, including the interest on those loans, so I'm not sure why you are troubled.

"You know I need this money for my children to go to college, Mr. Wright. You know my sons are going to be doctors and I will pay for their education. Why shouldn't I help others in the meantime?

"I helped a young man whose horse died buy a truck so he could make deliveries to his customers. I helped another buy the inventory he needed to start a new business. Both are doing well. Now I want to help the Johnsons buy a house for themselves and their children."

"I know, Mrs. Dreizen, but the Johnsons are a risk. They may not be able to pay it back."

"There is no risk in helping people, Mr. Wright. In the end, they are all we have."

37

The hot days of summer are finally waning. Al and Selig are playing ball in the backyard when I suddenly hear Al yelling. "Mama, Ann, Feggy, come quick!"

The sisters run outside with me close behind. Over near the garage, Selig's head appears to be missing—he has inserted it where a pane of glass had been just a minute before. Sharp shreds of glass surround his neck.

"What in the world happened here?"

Selig is crying so hard that Al has to explain. "We were playing ball and I hit one through the glass garage door. Selig tried to reach it by sticking his head through the hole."

I gesture to Ann and continue walking toward the garage. "Call the fire department."

"That's a good idea, Mama," responds Ann as she hurries back into the house. "They rescue people. They even rescue cats in trees."

"I'm not a cat in a tree," yells the headless Selig, and he proceeds to wail again. A fire truck rounds the corner, bells ringing. There is no blood insofar as I can see and nothing is on fire, so I will let the firemen do their jobs without my interference.

Because of all the noise, a crowd has begun to gather. I sit down on the back porch steps to catch my breath and to laugh at the fix Selig has gotten himself into.

I hear bells ringing in the distance and know there is a fire somewhere. Suddenly, Tateh bursts into the house and motions for Mamaleh and me to hide under the table in our small kitchen. There is a mob of men with torches in the street.

"What is burning, Tateh?" I whisper.

A tear runs down his face. "It is the synagogue, Boshka. They have set the synagogue on fire."

I cry too.

My attention returns to the present when I see Selig, freed from his temporary glass prison, running toward me. I inspect a tiny cut on his cheek and remind him to wash it well, and then thank the firemen for extracting my son. As I turn to go back into the house, I remind myself to ask Teddy to fix the window in the morning.

Lou and I have begun to spend more time together. He, Nora and Sam come almost every Sunday. We are back to eating lunch every day except for the occasional days I have to go into New York with Teddy to Teberg's to pick up wallpaper for a customer. On those days, Lou takes me to the Algonquin.

Once in a while we go out in the evenings without the children. Lou would go at least once every week if I'd agree, but it still makes me uneasy. I can't shake the feeling that I am dishonoring Nathan and I don't want people to gossip.

Lou says not to worry about what people say. He has waited this long, he says. He will wait some more. When I ask him how long he will wait, he says, "As long as it takes."

⊷═◉◉═⊶

The day of Al's bar mitzvah finally arrives. Max and Helen come from Attleboro and Jack and Sylvie from Yonkers. Miriam, Simon and their children come from New Orleans to attend, as do Lou and his children, our old friends from Anshe Sholom and our new friends from the Hebrew Institute. Even Mrs. Murphy accepts my invitation, though she's nervous because she's never been to a bar mitzvah before.

I'm amused, but I understand. "There's nothing to do, Mrs. Murphy. Al will read from the Torah. All you have to do is listen, be proud of him and then eat."

"Oh," she says and laughs. "Like with my own children at their First Communion."

Of course, Al makes us all proud—stumbling over only one Hebrew word. In his new suit and his tallis and yarmulke, he looks so much like Nathan I can't help but think how pleased he would have been!

Our children are turning into young men and women before my eyes. Al and Ann will be leaving Trinity School and attending Isaac E. Young—the new junior high school. Even though some of the exterior work needs to be completed, it will open on time for the beginning of the school year.

Before we can turn around, it is winter again, and though it is cold, our enthusiasm isn't diminished at all as we stand on the steps of the new synagogue at the Hebrew Institute on Union Avenue. With our friends and neighbors, we watch as the rabbi blesses the synagogue and opens the door with his key. We've waited a long time for this day—if only Nathan were here with us.

⊷═◯═⊶

In a few short months, the 1920s will be over. Lou has been trying to talk me into investing some of the money I've saved instead of renting theaters and co-signing on mortgages. "I don't think it's a good idea for people in New Rochelle to owe you so much money," he says. "You can't keep this up."

I am annoyed with him. "It's business, Lou. I give people a down-payment for a small mortgage and co-sign with them if I have to. So far, combined with profits from the business, I've been able to put away enough money so that all four of my children will be able to go to college. I want Al and Selig to go on to medical school after that."

Lou is aghast. "You didn't tell me that you actually hold the mortgage on houses of people you don't even know!"

"I didn't see that it was any of your concern. I don't mean to hurt your feelings, but I know what I'm doing."

He sighs. "Why don't you let me take some of your money and invest it in the stock market for you? I didn't make all my money in coffee and tea. The stock market is at an all-time high—you could double your investment in no time."

"No, Lou. I'll feel better if it is in the bank."

"I'm not your Nathan, Bessie, but I am your best friend. You know I would never do anything to hurt you."

I admit it sounds like a good idea, and Lou does have plenty of money—he certainly seems to know what he's doing. Doubling the money would not only allow me to pay for the children's educations, but would give me a good start toward my retirement. I am almost as old as Nathan was when he died and I don't want to be a burden on my children. I relent and give him a bank check for $25,000.

⋆⟶◉⟵⋆

I'm sitting in Nathan's favorite living room chair, listening to the radio. It's now late October and for three straight days, the stock market has fallen by record percentages. People are jumping out of windows. Long lines of people wait to withdraw their money from the banks. I don't understand all that is happening, but I do understand enough to know that every penny of the money I gave Lou is gone. Every penny.

--=◦=--

"Tateh, why can't we go to Vilna more often? There is so much more to do in Vilna than here in Glubokoye!"

"We don't have the money, Boshka. It takes most of what we make to keep the Russians happy and Max out of the army."

I pout and Tateh smiles. "Boshka, it's only money. You will see. Money comes and goes like the wind. People are all that matter."

--=◦=--

The door opens and someone rushes in. It's Lou.

"Bessie, you heard? Oh my God, Bessie, I'll pay you back. I will make sure your children are able to go to college and Al and Selig to medical school."

I know that Lou couldn't have known. He hasn't lost everything. Nor have I. I still have the house and my children. And the business.

I close my eyes again. It's only money, I tell myself.

"Bessie, I know your heart is breaking. So is mine. I feel so guilty. I should never have told you what to do."

I open my eyes and look at him. "You didn't twist my arm—I gave you the money. Life will go on. I'm still young enough to put more money in the bank—and I will work as long as I have to. Besides, I still have the interest from my loans. I'll be fine."

He leaves and for a week, I hear nothing from him. I call his office and his home but get no answer. I'm about to have Teddy drive me to Washington Heights to see what's wrong when I hear the back door open and I hear Lou's voice. "Bess, where are you?"

231

"I'm in the kitchen."

He strides into the room and lays a roll of bills on the table. "Here's part of the money I owe you," he says. "Next week I'll have more."

I protest, but to no avail. He will not take no for an answer.

"Bess, you know that I still have plenty of money. I won't be able to live with myself if I don't pay you back every penny." He leaves and I tuck the money away in a hiding place for safekeeping.

Suddenly tired, I go to my room to lie down until the children come home. I glance at the pillow and sigh. Where is that peace you promised now?

Business drops some but not so much that I'm not busy. I am fortunate that Nathan was forward-looking enough to go where some of the wealthiest families settled. He was right—they continue to invest in real estate and not just the stock market. There are some who will always have money and they will always need painting done, new wallpaper hung.

After the crash, I don't have to let a single worker go and of that I am proud. I will save enough at least to pay for the boys to go to college, but medical school—that is another thing.

38

⊰═◉═⊱

It's been four years since Black Tuesday. I've been able to replace almost half my loss. The Depression continues and everyone is nervous, even those not affected by the crash. President Hoover was widely blamed for it, which is probably why Franklin Roosevelt defeated him in the election.

⊰═◉═⊱

Tateh left us last year. A postcard came in the mail today with a photograph of my brother, Eliyahu, standing by Tateh's tombstone. The writing on the card was in Yiddish: "A memento from your brother after your father's death…"

I have only one image of my father. It's a sketch I have carried with me from Glubokoye. I've placed it on my dresser so I will never forget his face.

⊰═◉═⊱

Max has come from Attleboro and Jack from Yonkers. It's been only a matter of months since we heard the news of Tateh's passing and we're sitting shiva again. Mamaleh's broken heart could not go on.

My mother was one of the few women in Glubokoye who could read and write. The other women often went to Mamaleh for advice—they will have to find someone else to turn to.

So will I.

39

❧

A l is starting his third year at New York University. Who could have guessed he would buckle down like he has? Nathan would never have believed it—our prankster has turned into quite a student. The first year was a little challenging, however.

Once, a letter came from one of Al's professors saying he was failing one of his classes. No one was around to drive me into the city, so I grabbed my pocketbook and headed for the train station. I got off the subway at Washington Square and marched straight to Dr. Watson's office. I opened the door and there in a chair in the professor's office was Al.

"Mama, what are you doing here?"

"I got this letter in the mail today."

I shook hands with Dr. Watson and introduced myself. "I'm Mrs. Dreizen, Al's mother. What does this letter mean? Al is a smart boy. He's going to graduate from college. Then he'll go to dental school. He'll be the best dentist in New Rochelle, or maybe Pelham or Larchmont or Scarsdale. How can he be failing a course?"

"Please sit down, Mrs. Dreizen."

Al's face flushes. "Why are you here? You're embarrassing me. I can take care of this."

"Because I'm your mother and if you're failing something, I have to know why."

Dr. Watson has watched us with amusement and finally interrupts. "Mrs. Dreizen, Al is an excellent student, and I'm sure he will be a fine dentist. This letter has to do with a music course he's taking. He took it as an elective. I guess music is not his strength, but there's no need to worry. He's not becoming a musician."

I am not amused. "I sent him to New York University for you to tell me that? I'm paying all this money for him to take a music class? You should have asked me. Years ago, he wanted to play the piano, so I bought a used piano. Did he practice on it? No. Once in a while he would lie on the piano bench and play it with his feet."

Professor Watson thought the situation so humorous and that I was so funny that he offered to take Al and me to dinner. Late that night, when I got home, I told my other children that when they got older they could tell their friends that their mother went through NYU when Al was there.

Ann continues to help me with office work. I don't know what I will do when she marries and moves away. Feggy and Selig are still at home, but Feggy will graduate from New Rochelle High School this year.

Jack and Sylvie and their two daughters are doing well. Though sales are down, their stationery store is still turning a profit. His emphysema sometimes gives him a problem but he is still able to work.

Max was just elected president of the American Legion post in Attleboro. I've never asked him about what happened when he fought in the war. I suspect trying to describe it is like telling my children about the pogroms—unless you were there to see it all, it is hard to understand. Besides, who wants to revisit terror?

We hear on the radio that workers are striking in different parts of the country. Violence often accompanies them. Fortunately, the labor unrest hasn't affected me or my workers, although many in New Rochelle continue to suffer because of the Depression.

As a businesswoman, I can see both sides. Paying the workers is a large expense but, as I've said before, they must be treated with respect. If the tragedy of the Triangle Shirtwaist Factory taught us nothing else, it was that. If the unions can protect people like Rachael and others who live in squalor on the Lower East Side, I'm glad. But violence always frightens me—the emotional scars of the pogroms will never completely go away.

40

New Rochelle
1936

⊷═◉═⊶

Selig bounces up the steps with the mail. "Ann, there's a letter for you and it's from Pennsylvania. Who's Abe Bress?"

Before I can open my mouth, Feggy answers. "You remember, Selly. Mama knew them back in Glubokoye. When Papa died, Abe and his mother and sister came up on the train from Pennsylvania to the funeral."

Al, home for the weekend from college, snatches the letter from his brother's hand. "That can't be for Ann. Abe is *my* friend."

"It's addressed to *Ann*," says Feggy as she snatches it back and gives it to her sister. "Open it. Open it. What does it say?"

Ann tears open the envelope and proceeds to read. She blushes and then looks up at me with a blank expression. "He wants to see me and he's bringing a friend for Feggy. They want us to go to Playland with them."

I smile. "Good. He'll make a good husband—he went to college and is a teacher somewhere. Oh, dear, when did he say he's coming? I'll go over to the butcher and get a nice roast. I'll make roasted potatoes with it and…"

Ann is not amused. "Mama, I'm not getting married. I'm only nineteen."

"I was just a year older when I married your father. You're so picky with boys—you'll be 41 before you get married if I know you."

I turn to Al and Selig. "When they come, they'll sleep in your room."

Abe and his friend come as planned, and during the year, he returns numerous times. I know the relationship has become quite serious when Ann is invited for an extended visit to East Stroudsburg. I am reminded of Miriam and New Orleans.

By August, I am hosting an engagement party and planning a November wedding. We will spare no expense, just as Nathan would have insisted.

"Mama, I don't want such a big wedding," complains Ann.

"When *your* daughters get married," I say, "you can do what you want. Now, I'll do what *I* want."

⊷⊜⊶

The engagement party over, Ann and Al drive Abe and his parents to the train station. When they return to the house, I am heating some of the leftovers from the party. Ann sits down at the kitchen table—the rest of the children are scattered throughout the house. I smile to myself—it has been a while since I've had everyone here at the same time.

"Was Abe upset that you didn't go back with them?" I ask.

"Oh, no. He's busy helping his parents with the hotel and the sporting goods store next door. I don't know why he became a teacher—he loves that store."

"I'm glad. Abe's a good man and I'm so happy for you. As soon as you leave for Pennsylvania, though, I don't know what I'll do. Al's already moved out." I remove my shoes and rub my feet. "And then there's Feggy. She's dating that pharmacist Harry Goldman. He'll make a good husband…and a good living. The next thing I know she'll be gone and Selig will be gone and I'll be alone."

Ann pulls out another chair and points to it. "Sit with me, Mama. I've been meaning to talk to you about that very thing. Papa died when I was nine years old. But I'm 21 now. It was a long time ago."

She looks out the window into the backyard. "I know you still miss him. I miss him too. Even now I daydream that he's going to drive up the driveway in that black Model T filled with toys for the four of us."

"I'm sorry I never had time to shop for toys like Papa."

"You gave us other gifts, Mama. You gave us the gift of compassion."

"Compassion! You mean, like for opera singers who can't sing?"

Ann giggles. "Yes, Mama, you got us into some odd situations—like selling tickets for his very first and thankfully last concert. That *was* a disaster." She paused. "But you also sent the sewing machines and patterns to your cousins in Glubokoye and you took us with you to deliver food to the orphanage on holidays.

You collected money for the Steinhouse boy. We knew that if he hadn't had that operation, he would've died."

I poured myself a cup of coffee and sat down. I thought of the Steinhouses. "I knew what it was like to lose a child. I had to do something."

"I know, Mama. You've taken care of everybody except yourself. Now it's time to take care of you."

"What do you mean?"

"I may as well just say it, Mama. Why won't you marry Mr. Schaffer? I know he's asked you a hundred times since Mrs. Schaffer died."

"Because it would be like betraying your papa. Nathan never liked Lou."

"Why in the world would Papa like Lou? Papa knew Lou was in love with you. He was jealous. And why wouldn't he have been?"

"But I didn't marry Lou. I married Papa."

"You married Papa because you fell in love with Papa. You didn't fall in love with Mr. Schaffer then, but I know you love him now. He sure does love you."

It's my turn to look out the window. "Ann, you know I thank your papa every day for the business. I think you know that I'm not like most women—I need to be more involved in...well...life. I don't know how happy I would ever have been just cooking and cleaning and gossiping with the ladies."

I stop and gaze at my beautiful daughter. "Don't think I'm not thankful for my children, especially you. You were there for me from the moment your papa died."

"And I'll be here for you now." She hesitates. "Perhaps not to help you so much with the business, but here."

"What are you talking about?"

"Um, well, I was going to wait and tell you after the wedding, but I might as well go ahead. Abe and I are thinking of opening a toy store somewhere near here."

Before I can respond to this news, she continues.

"Mama, marry Mr. Schaffer. You'll have him to help you, and you'll still be able to help people in New Rochelle. You'll be able to help people *beyond* New Rochelle. And you'll still have the business."

"But…"

"But what? What's stopping you?"

"What about Al and Feggy and Selig? What will happen to them?"

"Mama, it's not like the state can take them away."

I take a sip of my coffee.

A hint of a smile appears on Ann's face. "But I'll have to admit that I'll never forget you and that broom the day Uncle Melvin showed up."

Both of us burst out laughing. When we finally compose ourselves, I see tears in Ann's eyes.

"Mama," she says, "that was a long time ago. We're all grown. I'm marrying the most wonderful man in the world. Al is in love with Estelle. Feggy will probably marry her pharmacist, and Selig is so cute that some girl is going to grab him as soon as he's out of dental school. The question isn't what's going to happen to *us*."

Together we carry the food to the dining room and the rest of my children begin to gather around the table. I go to my room to change into more comfortable clothes when I hear more laughter. By the time

I get downstairs, they are holding their stomachs with tears running down their faces.

"What is going on in here?" I ask.

Ann shakes her head. "Oh, Mama, Al was just telling about the time Selig stuck his head through the garage window and then couldn't get it out and the firemen had to come."

Selig pretends he's offended. "Don't you act like you're so smart, Annie. You're the one who punched Mary Wilson when she said Papa's truck was hers."

Al grins from ear to ear. "Yeah, I was going to hit her, but Annie beat me to it."

The room explodes again.

Next comes the story of Feggy's summer of sickness with her Uncle Max. "I was better after a week," she says, "but I was having so much fun, I didn't want to come home, so I pretended I was sick until it was time to go back to school.

"Speaking of having fun," she continues, "remember when Ann got her drivers' license and we told Mama we were picking up our friends to take them to school when we were *really* going to the picture show? And the time Mama made fun of Ann and said that she loved driving so much she wondered if she was going to drive to the bathroom?"

One after the other, the stories keep coming until finally, I excuse myself and go back to my bedroom to freshen up. I sit down on the side of the bed and pull Nathan's pillow into my lap.

‑‑❮❯‑‑

"Tateh," I ask, "were you very sad when Lillian's mother died?"

He flicked the reins and nodded his head. "Yes, Boshka. Of course."

"Then why did you marry Mamaleh? Wasn't it a dishonor to her?"

"To go on is not to dishonor the dead, Boshka. Life is for the living."

I am quiet, pondering his response, when he speaks again. "Besides, if I hadn't, I wouldn't have you. Think of all the joy I would have missed."

‑‑❮❯‑‑

I hear Feggy calling. "Mama, we're sitting down for dinner!"

I open the closet door and reach way in the back for a tattered old carpetbag—one of the two I carried from Glubokoye.

"Mama, your blintzes are getting cold!" yells Ann.

I cradle the pillow in my arms and press it gently to my lips. And then I put it into the bag, just as I did on that street in Vilna so long ago. I return the bag to its place in the closet and linger for a moment at the door.

"Nathan," I whisper as I close the door, "I will always love you."

‑‑❮❯‑‑

I embark on a brand new journey.

Afterword

⊷═◉═⊷

Bessie's Pillow is based on a series of conversations between my grandmother, Bessie Markman, and my mother, Ann Bress, around 1950. The events are all true—my grandmother did, indeed, meet my grandfather because of a pillow given to her at the train station in Vilna, Lithuania in 1906. The majority of stories told within really happened as well, from the destruction of all photographs following Nathan's death to her trip to NYU to find out why my uncle was failing a class, though the names of all secondary characters were changed in some way out of respect for the privacy of their families.

However, because 60 years have passed since those conversations took place, both changes in culture and tradition have impacted our memories. Please excuse any errors of fact or interpretation—they are all unintentional. Despite any that exist, I am satisfied, as was my mother, who lived to see the first draft of this novel finished, that the story honors the spirit of Bessie Markman and all those who came to America to escape persecution abroad. Despite hardship of varying kinds and degrees, most found joy in spite of it.

"Tateh," Rabbi Joseph Markman died in 1932. What happened to Sarah Markman—"Mamaleh"—is unknown, although my mother Ann remembered Bessie sitting shiva after receiving notification that she had died as well.

Then, in 1943, in the midst of WWII, the Nazis set fire to the ghetto in Glubokoye. Five thousand Jews would die in the conflagration. It is assumed that Bessie's two youngest brothers were among them, as they were never heard from again.

Bessie's brother Max and his wife Helen remained and prospered in Attleboro, Massachusetts, where he became the head of the local American Legion. He died in the early 1960's. His name is associated with a number of charitable institutions to this day. Jack and Sylvie sold their store in Yonkers and moved back to New Rochelle, where he was actively involved with Beth El Synagogue (formerly the Hebrew Institute). He lived into his late 70's.

Al and Selig would, in fact, both graduate from college and go on to become dentists. Al opened a practice in the Pintard Building in New Rochelle. After completing dental school, Selig served as a captain in the army in the Pacific theater during WWII. He came home, after the war, to join Al's dental practice in New Rochelle.

Interestingly, many residents of New Rochelle would never know Selig by his legal name. Instead, he would go by the initials "C. B." The "C" stood for "Cellock," a derivation of his name given to him by his first grade teacher. The "B" was for Bessie—he had no middle name.

Florence (Feggy) would indeed marry her pharmacist, Harold Goldman. Harry, one of nine children, served in WWII as a pharmacist in London and became the owner of a pharmacy in the Heathcote section of Scarsdale. A lover of flowers all her life, Feggy was an award-winning member of the Temple Israel Garden Club.

Ann and Abe (Bress) eventually opened a toy store on the same block as Harry's pharmacy. They had two daughters—Norma Bress Fleischman and me. When I was eleven, we (and Selig and his family) moved a few miles north to Eastchester, where Uncle Al and his family had already relocated, leaving only Feggy and Harry and their children in New Rochelle.

Although he was the youngest of Bessie's four children who survived to adulthood, Selig would be the first to go. In May 1970, he died of a massive heart attack just like my grandfather Nathan. Tragically, we would lose Jack in August and Al in April of the next year. Suffice it to say that was a very difficult time for our family.

Despite developing heart disease herself, secondary to damage sustained during her bout with rheumatic fever, Feggy would live into her 80's. And Ann, my mother, the driving force behind *Bessie's Pillow*, died in September 2012, at the age of 97.

When it fell to Bessie to operate her husband's contracting business, she abandoned her study for citizenship. She did not give up the dream, however, and would finally become an American citizen in 1944.

Bessie would never marry Lou, but they would remain close friends until, after suffering a series of strokes, she would journey, on February 12, 1951, to be with her beloved Nathan once again. She was 63.

What happened to the pillow? We're still trying to track it down. But, wherever it is, even if it resides only in the hearts and minds of those who remember, we trust that it continues to provide comfort.

May it bring you peace.

Linda Bress Silbert
May 2013

At the wedding of a friend in Manhattan
L-R: Selig, Ann, Bessie, Feggy, and Al

The Dreizens at home
L-R: Ann, Feggy, Bessie, Al and Selig

Rabbi Joseph Markman (Tateh)
Bessie brought this sketch of her father with her
in 1906. Until the day she died, it remained
on her dresser.

Sarah Markman (Mamaleh)
Discovered among family photos during the writing
of the book, the woman in the photo above is believed
to be Bessie's mother. No other photos of her exist.

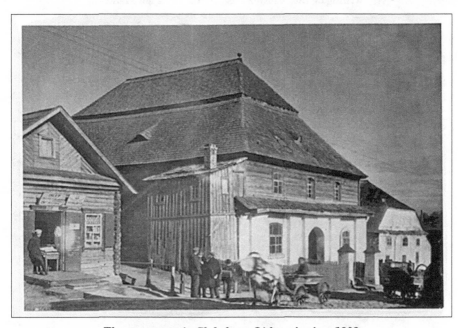

The synagogue in Glubokoye, Lithuania circa 1902
(Used with permission from Eilat Gordin Levitan and Larry Kotz
http://www.eilatgordinlevitan.com/)

Above left: One of Bessie's younger brothers
Above right: Bessie's brother Jack with the author, 1952
Below: The postcard apprising Bessie of her father's death.
The writing on the headstone reads: "Rabbi Joseph Markman"

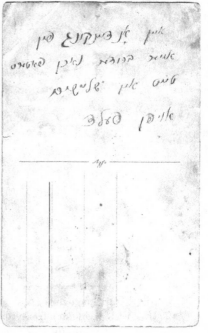

Above: The boys, Al & Selig (Cellock)
Left: The girls, Feggy and Ann, strolling in
East Stroudsburg, Pa.

Right: Ann, Cellock & Feggy
Below: Feggy, Al & Ann

Above: Ann Dreizen on a pony brought to Trinity School, New Rochelle.
Below: Isaac E. Young Junior High School in the late 1920s—on Pelham Rd.

The author's father, Abe Bress
at one year - 1911

Feggy, Ann and Abe Bress (behind Ann) with friends
at Playland in Rye, NY on August 9, 1936, the day of
Ann and Abe's engagement party.

**The hotel in East Stroudsburg, Pa. that was
owned by Abe Bress' parents**

**Ann and Abe out for a walk
in East Stroudsburg, 1938**

Above: Al and Abe in top hats and tails for Al's wedding, 1941
Below: Harry Goldman and Norma Bress Fleischman, 1942

Bessie's America

*B*essie's Pillow was enhanced by research about the political and cultural environment in which Bessie Markman Dreizen lived. Throughout the book, people, places and events in the New York area and beyond were mentioned. The book version contains some of the main categories from the more complete "Bessie's America" that appears on the website *www.BessiesPillow.com*. We've also included here some links to the many wonderful resources that appear on the website.

Beginning with a brief summary describing the political and social environments in Eastern Europe that drove hundreds of thousands to immigrate to America in the late 19th / early 20th centuries, Bessie's America provides a multimedia, interactive guide to the America Bessie and her fellow immigrants would discover. Newsreels, songs, movie clips, photographs and even a recipe or two will take you back in time.

Eastern European Immigration
and the Progressive Era

Beginning in 1881, two million Eastern European Jews would come to America, the largest number from the Russian Pale of Settlement (Lithuania, Belarus, Moldavia, the Ukraine, and parts of Poland).

In 1906 alone, 215,665 Russian Jewish immigrants passed through Ellis Island on their way to New York City. Five out of six would remain in New York. By 1910 almost half a million Russian immigrants lived in the city.

The numbers of immigrants, especially Russian Jews and southern Italians, shocked Congress. With the fear of "foreign elements" taking over the country, President Calvin Coolidge signed the Immigration Act of 1924. Although limiting immigrants from many countries, those from Eastern Europe would be affected the most.

By then, however, the demographics of New York had already changed from the pretense of homogeneity to the cosmopolitan city it soon would be known for.

Many East Europeans would leave from Hamburg or other ports in Germany en route to New York where third class passengers would go through immigration inspections at Ellis Island or Castle Garden. Others would travel to Boston, Philadelphia, and even as far west as Chicago.

As described, the immigrants came to escape the cruel and violent pogroms of czarist Russia, the restrictions placed on Jews, and the poverty of life in the shtetles. They came for the economic opportunities they believed America would offer, some for free education.

Although most came with their families, Boshka Markman came alone in 1906. Just 18 years old, she left her parents and four younger brothers behind in Glubokoye, Lithuania. As was common, she would also leave behind her Russian name in preference for the more "American" name, Bessie.

Unlike most, Bessie was fortunate enough to travel first class. Most of her orthodox contemporaries in Lithuanian shtetles married men who had been chosen for them, were allowed only 3-4 years of

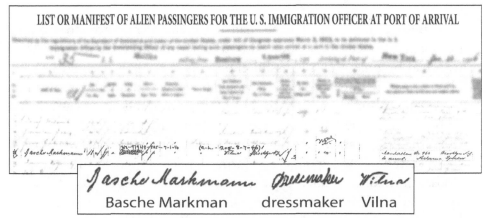

LIST OR MANIFEST OF ALIEN PASSINGERS FOR THE U. S. IMMIGRATION OFFICER AT PORT OF ARRIVAL

Basche Markman   dressmaker   Vilna

**Image derived from the actual manifest of Bessie's voyage from Hamburg.
Note the Germanic adaptation of her name.**

school, and expected to act in obedience to their rabbis, fathers, or husbands. Bessie, with the support of her parents, broke out of this tradition.

The majority of Russian Jews on Bessie's ship jammed into the hot and unsanitary steerage area. Families, often with babies and young children, came onto the ship with the clothes on their backs, a few belongings, and enough kosher food they hoped would last the trip. Some would die before the journey ended.

Speaking no English and accustomed to the slower pace of the "Old World," the immigrants would find themselves startled at the hustle and bustle of New York and frustrated by the language barrier. And, unlike the earlier immigrants from Western Europe, they had never lived under a democracy.

The poorest families would settle on the Lower East Side, living in crowded, unhealthy tenements. Not allowed to own land in Russia, the immigrants would often come with skills such as those needed in the needle trades. So, not surprisingly, these workers would flock to menial jobs in the garment industry as ready-made clothing became popular. Others would sell from pushcarts. Entire families would work at home in the cigar industry.

The Lower East Side would become a center of Yiddish community, culture, and food, drawing Jews from the city and suburbs to Yiddish theater and kosher delicatessens.

Bessie's America

Bessie, on the other hand, had the financial resources to avoid tenement life and would live with friends in Washington Heights who had become even successful enough to employ household help. Throughout her life, however, she would be drawn back to her roots in the Yiddish community, attending a Yiddish movie and eating pastrami on black rye or cherry blintzes with sour cream after the show.

The Progressive era, in full swing in 1906, brought about sweeping social activism and political reform. Under President Theodore Roosevelt, reform-minded politicians and citizens would push to rid local politics of corruption and big business of monopolies. Settlement houses, often run by Jewish reform-minded men and women, would help the poor. Henry Street Settlement on New York's Lower East Side emphasized health and sanitation. Jane Addams' Hull House in Chicago offered free kindergarten, recreation programs for children, and night classes for adults.

Union activism would rise out of this concern for improving the lives of all citizens. As the Jewish immigrants discovered the low wages, long hours, the horrors of child labor, and the dreadful working conditions, some would become active in the rising labor movement. Woman Suffrage and Prohibition would both become law in 1920.

By the 1920s even women's fashion had changed drastically. Bessie arrived in America wearing a modest, if cumbersome, full-skirted floor-length dress with a high neck and long sleeves. Almost overnight, daring young women would begin wearing dresses with lower necklines, shorter skirts and no sleeves. By the 1930s more conservative women like Bessie would wear short-sleeved cotton housedresses falling a couple of inches below the knee. An apron kept splatters from soiling a clean dress. For many, evening wear would remain floor length.

Baseball, radio and movies, unheard of in Eastern Europe, became popular pastimes in all but the most religious households. Instead of the often gender-segregated exuberant dancing in the "Old Country," young people scandalized their grandparents by dancing with their arms around each other.

Immigrants, eager to become "Americanized," would learn English, become citizens, vote, start businesses, and go to school. No matter where they stood on reform issues and politics, few would return to Eastern Europe. Those few who wanted to go back would be deterred by wars and upheaval in Europe. They would stay and raise their children as American citizens.

An Interactive Multimedia Guide

Bessie's Pillow takes place between 1906, when Bessie comes to America and 1936, when Bessie and Nathan's older daughter Ann is engaged to Abe Bress. Below you'll find links to radio shows the family listened to, theater they enjoyed, music they knew, desserts they ate at restaurants, and political events and social changes that would affect them and others of the time.

The audios are digitized recordings taken from Edison cylinders and other early recordings. It's a scratchy sound compared to audio quality of the 21st century. Reporters and speakers on radio shows and in newsreels may speak slowly, often with long pauses when a reporter is describing a live event. Newsreels are in black and white.

Immigration Resources

Ellis Island and How to Look Up Your Ancestors: The largest number of people arriving in America from Europe during the years 1892 to 1954 would enter through Ellis Island as Bessie did. Now operated by the National Park Service as an historic sight and museum, you can look for your ancestors in the Ellis Island records at the Park. Or use the online database at *www.BessiesPillow.com/ellisisland*

Hebrew Aid Societies: Upon arriving in New York, Jewish men would form groups with other men from their town with the purpose of providing fellowship and help for others from their area. Bessie would find Nathan through the membership records for the Glubokoye Society. See the listing for Nathan's death in the original Glubokoye Society records at *www.BessiesPillow.com/hebrewaid*

Bessie's America

Other immigrant stories: A classic, first published in 1925 and republished in 2003, *Bread Givers*, a novel by Anzia Yezierska, tells the story of a young Polish immigrant woman who lives with her Hasidic Jewish family on the Lower East Side and struggles to become an independent woman. (New York: Persea Books, 2003)

After spending her childhood in the Pale in Lithuania, Mary Antin immigrated to Boston with her family in 1895. In her 1912 autobiography *The Promised Land*, Mary describes living in Boston as a Russian Jewish immigrant and her passion for school as a way out of poverty. Read Antin's book online at *www.BessiesPillow.com/antin*

Tenement Museum: See how immigrants lived in a typical tenement building on the Lower East Side in New York. Built in 1863, more than 7,000 immigrants lived at 97 Orchard St. from 1863 to 1935. The restored tenement displays apartments from different time periods.

Located at 103 Orchard St. between Delancey and Broome, the Tenement Museum offers tours of the tenement, talks, walking tours, and resources to individuals, groups, and schools. See: *www.tenement. org*

TransAtlantic Steamships: Bessie, Nathan, Nathan's brothers and sister, Lou, Miriam, Max, and Jack would cross the Atlantic on large ocean liners to come to America. Many of Bessie's neighbors and all of her friends at Anshe Sholom would also come by steamship. Bessie and her brothers sailed on the Hamburg-American line. Diagrams of this company's ships, travel brochures, pictures of the rooms, even menus can be seen. Visit: *www.BessiesPillow.com/ship*

Immigrants would be medically cleared before being allowed on the ship. See a typical immigration inspection card at *www. BessiesPillow.com/card*

Famous People

Babe Ruth: The passion for baseball included devotion to its stars. Babe Ruth, the most famous baseball player in American history, hit 2,174 home runs and was a seven-time World Series champion from 1915 through 1932. His 1920 New York Yankees jersey sold for $4.4 million dollars. Read the biography of this colorful ball player and check his statistics: *www.BessiesPillow.com/baberuth*

Emma Lazarus and the Statue of Liberty: The famous lines, "Give me your tired, your poor, your huddled masses yearning to breathe free" appear in the sonnet "The New Colossus" on a plaque at the base of the Statue of Liberty. Written by Emma Lazarus, a Jewish American poet, in 1883, as a contribution to an auction to help raise money for the construction of the statue, the poem would not appear on the statue until 1903. Read the "The New Colossus" at the beginning of *Bessie's Pillow*.

The Statue of Liberty was sculpted by Frederic Auguste Bartholdi in France in 1884 and arrived in New York Harbor on a French frigate in 1885. Its 350 individual pieces had been packed in 214 crates before being shipped.

Take a virtual tour of the Statue of Liberty at *www.BessiesPillow. com/liberty-tour*. The statue is so large that the length of her right arm is 42 feet. For more details and statistics about the Statue of Liberty, see *www.BessiesPillow.com/liberty-creation*

Charles Lindbergh: On May 20, 1927, Charles Lindbergh flew from New York to Paris, the first person to fly across the Atlantic Ocean alone. The trip took 33½ hours. His reception in Washington, DC, including a march down Pennsylvania Avenue and a reception at the foot of the Washington Monument, was broadcast live on the radio. Watch a National Geographic documentary on Charles Lindbergh and his flight to Paris: *www.BessiesPillow.com/lindbergh*

Thomas Paine and the American Revolution: Common Sense, a pamphlet that helped convince the colonists to revolt against Great Britain, was written by Thomas Paine, a Revolutionary War hero who lived in New Rochelle from 1802 until 1806. Paine's cottage, a National Historic Landmark, is located at 20 Sicard Avenue. The site also includes the first school house in New Rochelle, a museum, and the Thomas Paine Memorial. All are open to the public. Today, Girl Scouts continue to meet in the "Little House" between the Thomas Paine Cottage and the Thomas Paine Memorial House. Read the text of the pamphlet "Common Sense" online: *www.BessiesPillow.com/commonsense*

Food and Recipes

Baked Alaska and How to Make It: Flaming desserts, first at Peaberrys in New Rochelle and later at the Algonquin Hotel in New York, startled Bessie. Because of their dramatic appearance, these easy-to-create novelties gained great popularity. To fix baked Alaska, cover ice cream with meringue and toast the meringue with a BBQ lighter. Then soak 3-4 sugar cubes in brandy or any liqueur, place the cubes on top of the toasted meringue and light them with the BBQ lighter. Now you're ready to serve a flaming dessert.

Since the liqueur quickly burns off, this is basically a non-alcoholic dessert. A chef at New Delmonico's named his concoction "Baked Alaska" to celebrate the American acquisition of Alaska in 1876.

Immigrant Recipes: Discover what immigrant mothers cooked for their families in *97 Orchard: An Edible History of Five Immigrant Families in One New York Tenement* by Jane Ziegelman (NY: Harper, 2011). Get German, Italian, Irish, Russian, and Kosher recipes that immigrant mothers used in poorly-equipped kitchens to feed large families.

Peach Melba: Named after Nellie Melba, Australian soprano whom Nathan and Bessie heard at Carnegie Hall, peach melba was created by the French chef Auguste Escoffier at the Savoy Hotel in London. It's easy, fast, and flameless. Put a scoop of vanilla ice cream in a bowl, cover with fresh sliced peaches, and pour raspberry puree or sauce on top of the peaches and ice cream.

Health

Communicable Diseases: Bessie's life-long concern that her children or her brothers might die wasn't mere paranoia caused by the loss of her husband and two children. Children and adults became seriously ill and often died of diseases easily cured today by drugs or prevented by vaccines.

Whooping cough, diphtheria, scarlet fever, tuberculosis, and polio were serious illnesses. Pneumonia, influenza, and even measles often took lives. The Spanish Flu Pandemic of 1918-1920 infected 500 million people world wide and killed approximately 75 million.

As in the story, Bessie lost two children to scarlet fever. Feggy suffered from rheumatic fever, and both Al and Selig would get polio. Nathan, Al, and Selig would all die from heart failure at relatively young ages. Those suffering from malnutrition and living in unsanitary conditions, such as Rachael and her family, would often die from tuberculosis. Bessie herself would suffer for many years from extremely high blood pressure which, coupled with several small strokes, would lead to her death in 1952.

Safety Standards: Without realizing the health hazards of these materials, Nathan and Bessie would store lead paint, asbestos and horsehair-based plaster in their shop for workers to use in people's homes. Many workers in the construction industry died of what would later be diagnosed as lead poisoning. Out of concern for her workers' safety, Bessie encouraged them to wash their hands frequently, though regulation of these products wouldn't occur until 1976. All three of these toxic materials can still be found in older homes and commercial buildings.

Movies

Silent films: Bessie and her family loved going to the movies and first saw silent films. Although actors didn't talk in silent films, the films were accompanied by music either in the film or played live on an organ in the theater itself. Popular silent films that would have played in New Rochelle included The Perils of Pauline with Pearl White (1914), Birth of a Nation directed by D. W. Griffiths (1915), The General with Buster Keaton (1927), and City Lights with Charlie Chaplin (1931).

Watch "Chapter One" of *The Perils of Pauline*:
www.youtube.com/watch?v=ZVPQa-10030

Watch *City Lights*:
www.vimeo.com/25622059

See popular silent films from 1903 through 1931:
www.filmsite.org/silentfilms2.html

Golden Age of Hollywood: The 1930s brought talking into the movies. Considered "The Golden Age of Hollywood," the films, usually in black and white, ranged from drama to comedy to westerns to the first cartoons. Bessie's family would watch a newsreel and a cartoon before the feature film. Movies included Tarzan, the Ape Man with Johnny Weissmuller, the Olympic swimming champion (1932); The Great Ziegfeld (1936) lasting 2 hours and 59 minutes with lots of singing and dancing (1936); Baby Burlesks, Shirley Temple's first movies (1933), and The Wise Little Hen, featuring the first appearance of Donald Duck (1934). Laurel and Hardy, the famous comedians who began their movie career with short silent films, made their first talking film, "Unaccustomed as We Are," in 1929.

Watch the trailer for The Great Ziegfeld:
www.imdb.com/title/tt0027698/

Laugh at Laurel and Hardy:
www.laurel-and-hardy.com/

See Donald Duck in *The Wise Little Hen*:
www.youtube.com/watch?v=A5dowCyaP7I

Read a history of movies in the 1930s:
www.filmsite.org/30sintro.html

Music and Dancing

Carnegie Hall and Nellie Melba: Built by Andrew Carnegie in 1891, Carnegie Hall quickly became the most popular concert hall in New York City. Far less expensive than the Metropolitan Opera, Carnegie hall offered an eclectic range of events. One could hear the New York Symphony conducted by Tchaikovsky or a lecture by Mark Twain. As early as 1895, comedy acts such as the Amateur Comedy Club had audiences laughing.

On their first date, Nathan and Bessie would hear the famous Australian soprano Nellie Melba at Carnegie Hall. Melba toast and the dessert peach melba are both named after her. Although her concerts focused on well-known arias from Italian and French opera, Melba included popular songs. Always a lady, she wore a hat and carried a small purse while recording "Home Sweet Home" in a studio:
www.BessiesPillow.com/melbasong

A BBC Fox Movietone newsreel of her half-mile long funeral procession in Melbourne in 1931 would be seen in movie theaters around the world including at Loew's and the RKO in New Rochelle:
www.BessiesPillow.com/melbafuneral

Dance Craze: From going to a sleazy dance hall on the Lower East Side to learning the latest dance at an uptown studio to dancing in a ballroom to the big bands, everybody danced.

Watch the Hesitation Waltz as Nathan and Bessie would have danced it before they were married. *www.BessiesPillow.com/hesitation*

Or how about a lesson in the Fox Trot?
www.BessiesPillow.com/foxtrot

Young couples loved animal dances such as the Grizzly Bear, but Nathan and Bessie would find them too risqué. *www.BessiesPillow.com/bear*

Glen Island and the Big Bands: Bessie celebrated her 19th birthday in 1906 with Nathan at Glen Island, one of the earliest amusement parks in the country. Glen Island closed in 1908 (see General Slocum below under "News"), reopening as a dance pavilion and speakeasy during prohibition.

After prohibition, Bessie's children and their spouses or dates would go to Glen Island to dance to the big band sounds of Ozzie Nelson (the same Ozzie of the TV sitcom "The Adventures of Ozzie and Harriet" fame), Les Brown, and the Dorsey Brothers. In 1939 Glenn Miller and his orchestra would get their start at Glen Island. Listen to some tunes from Ozzie Nelson's orchestra at *www.BessiesPillow.com/ozzienelson*

Musical Theater

45 Minutes from Broadway: Listen to Bill Murray, a popular early 20th century singer (no, not that one), in the title song from this George M. Cohan musical featuring New Rochelle. Nathan took Bessie to see this musical on one of their first dates. The digital recording is taken from an original Edison cylinder recording from 1906: *www.BessiesPillow.com/broadway*

Ragtime: Although not mentioned in *Bessie's Pillow*, this 1975 novel by E. L. Doctorow was set in New Rochelle. Winning two literary awards, the novel would later become a movie, and then a hit Broadway musical. Watch the preview for the musical: *www.BessiesPillow.com/ragtime*

Showboat: Musical theater focused on comedy and dancing until 1927 when Showboat opened on Broadway. The first musical with a coherent plot and songs, Showboat confronts gambling, poverty, and racism. Bessie, Lou, and their children would have many opportunities to see Showboat on Broadway and at the movies in New Rochelle. Paul Robeson, actor, singer, and civil rights activist, sang the role of Joe in American performances in 1932, 1936, and 350 times in London. See scenes from Showboat and listen to Robeson sing "Ol Man River": *www.BessiesPillow.com/robeson*

New Rochelle

Hebrew Institute and Beth El: Founded four years after Nathan and his friends started Anshe Sholom, the Hebrew Institute began as a Hebrew school. Bessie and her children celebrated the opening of the Hebrew Institute Synagogue, an orthodox congregation, in 1927. In 1931 the Hebrew Institute changed its name to Beth El. Beth El would become a conservative congregation in 1948. Three generations of the family would marry in one or the other synagogues. Read the story of Anshe Sholom, the Hebrew Institute, Beth El and other synagogues in New Rochelle at *www.BessiesPillow.com/synagogues*.

Left: Anshe Sholom, built 1904
Right: The Hebrew Institute, later Beth El
(photos courtesy of the New Rochelle Library)

The Huguenots: In 1688, 33 French Protestant families landed at what is now Hudson Park to found New Rochelle. One hundred years later Huguenots would still settle in New Rochelle. As the best known and largest French-speaking community north of New York City, families would send their children to New Rochelle to learn French. For an early history of the Huguenots in New Rochelle, download the free e-book version of New Rochelle through Seven Generations written by C. H. Augur in 1908: *www.BessiesPillow.com/nrgenerations*

Queen City of the Sound: New Rochelle boasted elegant homes, fine shopping, excellent schools, a quick commute into New York on the train, spacious parks, and memorials to war heroes from George Washington to those killed in World War I. The two movie theaters, Loew's and the RKO, could each seat more than 2,500 people.

For early pictures and a brief history of the "Queen City of the Sound," see Barbara Davis, *New Rochelle: Images of America* (Charleston, SC: Arcadia Publishing, 2009) and Barbara Davis, *New Rochelle: Postcard History Series* (Charleston, SC: Arcadia Publishing, 2012). The New Rochelle Public Library has some city archives and photographs online: *www.BessiesPillow.com/nrlibrary*.

Watch a video of New Rochelle's history: *www.BessiesPillow.com/newrochelle*

News

The General Slocum: With a church picnic planned, 1,342 people from Little Germany on the Lower East Side boarded the General Slocum excursion boat on Sunday afternoon, June 15, 1904. When the steamer caught fire and sank in the East River, 1,021 people drowned or died from the fire. Many families, frightened by the disaster, stopped taking steamers for Sunday outings. Excursion steamer companies, including John Starin's Glen Island steamer, went out of business within a few years.

The General Slocum disaster was the largest disaster in New York history until 9/11. The story is told in *Ship Ablaze: The Tragedy of The General Slocum* by Ed O'Donnell. (New York: Broadway Books, 2004). A short documentary includes pictures of the disaster: *www.BessiesPillow.com/slocum*

Model T Ford: In 1908 the first automobile rolled off a factory assembly line. Henry Ford's Model T, although too expensive at first for the average American, would eventually become affordable. By 1915, Ford had manufactured one million Tin Lizzies as Model Ts were nicknamed. Watch the Model T assembly line in action: *www.BessiesPillow.com/modelt*

From the Newspapers: In 1904, Nathan would read the *New Rochelle Press*. The November issue shows an ad for the Boston Spa, which would soon be serving ice cream to Bessie and her family: *www.BessiesPillow.com/newspaper1904*

The notice of Bessie's mortgage is listed in the 1918 issue of *The New Rochelle Pioneer*. See: *www.BessiesPillow.com/newspaper1918*

Panama Canal: The only way to reach the Pacific Ocean from the Atlantic Ocean was around the southern tip of South America. With the completion of the Panama Canal in 1914, a ship could make the trip in half the time which not only increased maritime trade and shipping but symbolized American power. Locks at each end lift ships up to Gatun Lake, 85 feet above sea-level. Watch the PBS "American Experience" episode on the Panama Canal: *www.BessiesPillow.com/panama*

Parks & Beaches

Hudson Park: In 1883 Alexander Hudson sold his Hudson Grove picnic area to the City of New Rochelle for $38,000. Going to Hudson Park quickly became a favorite weekend activity where Bessie's family would enjoy the beach and splashing in the Sound. When the family got hungry, they could get a quick snack or even supper at the refreshment pavilion. Rowing and yacht clubs built boat houses in the park, and the Rose Garden and bandstand with live music would draw summertime crowds.

See early pictures and postcards of Hudson Park: *www. BessiesPillow.com/hudsonpark*

Playland: This amusement park in Rye, NY was a favorite of Bessie's children. Although Playland opened in 1928, its famous Dragon Roller Coaster wasn't completed until the next season. The coaster, one of the few wooden roller coasters still in operation, boasts 3,400 feet of track and reaches 80 feet in height. At the top, riders get a quick look at the Long Island Sound.

The photograph on page 253 of Ann and Abe Bress with Feggy and friends on the day of their engagement was taken there.

The amusement park was added to the National Historic Register in 1987. Watch the opening-day film of the Dragon Coaster: *www. BessiesPillow.com/playland*

Influential Presidents during Bessie's Lifetime

Theodore Roosevelt (Republican, 1901-1909): When President William McKinley was assassinated in September 1901, Vice President Theodore Roosevelt became President. Despite his party affiliation as a Republican, Roosevelt would be known for progressive policies, legislation curtailing the power of monopolies, ecological conservation, doubling the number of national parks, and a Nobel Peace Prize for his contribution to ending the Russo-Japanese War. A video summary of Roosevelt's life can be seen at *www.BessiesPillow.com/troosevelt*

Bessie's children loved their teddy bears. Find out why teddy bears are named after Theodore Roosevelt: *www.BessiesPillow.com/teddy*

Woodrow Wilson (Democrat, 1913-1921): From President of Princeton University to President of the United States, Woodrow Wilson championed currency, credit and tariff reform and established the Federal Trade Commission. Wilson, strongly opposed to war, kept the United States out of World War I until April 6, 1917.

The war would end November 11, 1918. Wilson's "Fourteen Points" delivered in a speech to Congress outlined what he believed would ensure lasting peace and fairness among all nations. Read the Fourteen Points: *www.BessiesPillow.com/14points*

Veterans Day is celebrated on November 11 to honor not only those Americans who fought in World War I but all service veterans.

Listen to "Over There," one of the most popular songs during the war and watch the slide show of photographs and World War I posters: *www.BessiesPillow.com/overthere*

Herbert Hoover (Republican, 1929-1933): On October 29, 1929 the stock market crashed. The large drop in the value of stocks on this day caused thousands of people, including Bessie and Lou, to lose much, if not all, of their savings. It became known as "Black Tuesday."

The stock market crash was followed by hundreds of bank failures across the country as people rushed to withdraw their money. President Herbert Hoover, unable to stop the economic downturn of the Great Depression, would lose the next election to Franklin Roosevelt. That public opinion no longer backed Prohibition, which Hoover still supported, may have also contributed to Hoover's defeat. In addition, the death of several veterans during the Bonus Army protest lost Hoover the support of veterans of both parties. Watch a video about Black Tuesday: *www.BessiesPillow.com/1929crash*

Franklin D. Roosevelt (Democrat, 1933-1945): Millions lacked jobs and enough money to feed their families when Franklin D. Roosevelt became President. He soon offered his "New Deal," intended to deliver relief, recovery and reform. The New Deal successfully provided jobs for millions of Americans through programs like the Civilian Conservation Corps and the Works Progress Administration.

However, Roosevelt was unable to end the Great Depression. Ironically, it would be the mobilization for World War II what would bring back full employment and economic growth. Watch a newsreel of President Roosevelt's inauguration: *www.BessiesPillow.com/fdrinauguration*

Other Presidents included William H. Taft (Republican, 1909-1913), Warren Harding (Repubican, 1921-1923), and Calvin Coolidge (Republican, 1923-1929). Biographies of the Presidents can be found at *www.BessiesPillow.com/presidents*

Radio

Fireside Chats: Although Nathan heard stern and dry Calvin Coolidge on the radio during the 1924 presidential election, Franklin Roosevelt would popularize presidential radio broadcasts with his Fireside Chats. Bessie, always interested in politics, would continue to listen to Roosevelt on the radio in the years after Nathan died. Several Fireside chats are available at *www.BessiesPillow.com/fdrchat*

The Goldbergs: Listening to popular radio shows like "The Goldbergs," a serialized drama with lots of laughs, kept Bessie's spirits up. Beginning in 1929, the show centered around Jewish homelife in the Bronx. The Goldbergs made it to Broadway in the 1948 play "Me and Molly." The radio series became a television series running from 1949 to 1956, and a 1973 Broadway musical, "Molly." Unlike most comedies, "The Goldbergs" didn't shy away from serious issues such as World War II and Nazi Germany. Listen to radio episodes of "The Goldbergs" at *www.BessiesPillow.com/goldbergs*

NBC used Molly to help advertise Ecko kitchen products. She shows audiences her kitchen and states emphatically that she'd rather have a kitchen of Ecko housewares than a diamond bracelet: *www.BessiesPillow.com/mollyad*

Radio Popularity: By 1933, despite the ravages of the Great Depression, sixty percent of all American households would own radios for which they paid $47 or more. The 1930 U.S. census included a check box to indicate whether a family owned a radio or not. From the news to baseball, comedies to soap operas, westerns to murder mysteries, it was all on the radio. Listen to some radio shows Bessie and her family would have listened to at *www.BessiesPillow.com/radio*

Social Movements

Jacob Riis: A photographer and journalist, Jacob Riis published "How the Other Half Lives" in 1890, documenting the conditions of tenement house living similar to the way in which Rachel's family lived. Riis' book, along with pressure from other reformers, would spur the passage of the New York State Tenement House Act of 1901 which required better ventilation, improved hallway lighting, and indoor toilets. Read and see photographs from "How the Other Half Lives" at *www.BessiesPillow.com/riis*

Woman Suffrage: The 19th Amendment, giving women the right to vote, passed in 1920. Many women like Bessie would agree that women should vote but would think it improper to march in parades or participate in public demonstrations.

The opposition to woman suffrage diminished when President Wilson jailed demonstrators who had chained themselves to the white house gates. The outrage from the public and many in Congress over beatings, unsanitary conditions, and forced feeding in jail prompted Wilson to accept woman suffrage.

Carrie Chapman Catt, one of the most famous suffragists, lived in New Rochelle in an elegant Colonial Revival style home on Paine Ave. from 1927 until her death in 1947.

Watch a Sewell Belmont Museum documentary of the 1917 woman suffrage protest outside the White House at *www.BessiesPillow.com/suffrage-protest*

Vaudeville and Yiddish Theater

Eddie Foy and Vaudeville: From the 1890s through the 1920s, popular variety shows, called "vaudeville," could include comedy, music, dancers, magicians, trained animals, acrobats, plays, minstrels, and athletes. Bessie and her family loved the Jewish vaudeville on the Lower East Side in New York. (See Yiddish Theater and Molly Picon below.)

After crawling through a sewer to escape a Chicago theater fire which claimed 600 lives, Foy would move to New Rochelle. As mentioned, he and his family lived in "The Foyer," one of the largest homes Nathan's company would paint. "Eddie Foy and the Seven Little Foys" became one of the most popular vaudeville acts in America from 1910 to 1923. After Foy's death, the Foy family donated Foy's estate to New Rochelle. The Eddie Foy Park is located at Weyman Avenue and Pelham Road. In the 1955 movie, "The Seven Little Foys," Bob Hope played Eddie Foy. A TV remake of the movie would follow. *www.BessiesPillow.com/foytv* See Bob Hope and James Cagney's dance routine from the movie: *www.BessiesPillow.com/foymovie*

Yiddish Theater and Molly Picon: Jewish Families from around New York City and surrounding communities would flock to the Lower East Side to watch live theater, variety shows, vaudeville and movies in Yiddish. From serious drama to comedy, stars such as Molly Picon entertained audiences with stories that usually focused on immigrant life in America. Molly, whose career began with a vaudeville troupe, would appear on stage, in silent films, in the "talkies," and eventually on Broadway. True to her vaudeville background, Molly, a comedian, could sing, dance, play a variety of musical instruments and perform cartwheels, somersaults, head stands, and flying stunts.

Watch Molly and her friends dance in a 1923 clip from East and West (Ost und West). *www.BessiesPillow.com/mollypicon*. (Look for subtitles in English and Yiddish.) At 81, Molly wrote and toured with her one-woman show "Molly." See clips of her show here: *www.BessiesPillow.com/piconshow*

Boshka "Bessie" Markman Dreizen
(1887-1951)

Acknowledgments

First and foremost, I wish to thank my mother, Ann Dreizen Bress, who passed away shortly after the first draft of the manuscript was completed. She loved telling Bessie's story, and was thrilled to see it come to fruition.

Next, I wish to thank my husband, Al Silbert, Ed.D., who lovingly read and contributed to every draft and faithfully restored all of the family photographs for inclusion in the book.

Thanks are also due my children—Brian Silbert, Cheryl Schnitzer, Ph.D. and our son-in-law, Ted Schnitzer—for their continuous feedback and ongoing support, and my wonderful grandsons, Danny and Robby.

I thank the following relatives and their families as well, for helping with, names, dates and places, for reading drafts, or for just being supportive during this long journey: My sister and brother-in-law Norma and Charles Fleischman, my cousins Nancy and Paul Levy, Robert Goldman, M.D., Dianne and Marty Jaffe, Susan McCue, and Fred and Selma Moses.

Bessie's Pillow is richer because of the various questions and comments of the many people who listened to Ann's stories, read the original manuscript or helped with critiques, advice and dates—among them Peter McCardle, D.D.S. for his thoughts, words and writings; Robert Goldberg; Rabbi Eytan and Rebecca Hammerman; Loring Mandel; Staton Rabin; Bob Zaslow; Vera Sklaar; Cheryl Garani; Barbara Davis (New Rochelle's town historian); and Tom Geoffino and Larry Sheldon, director and historian, respectively, for the New Rochelle Library.

A very special thank you goes to: Jennifer Ciotti, for editing and revising the first draft; Vally Sharpe, for the final edit and interior layout; Frank Rivera, for cover design; and MaryJo Wagner, Ph.D. for her assistance in providing historical perspective and for developing the *Bessie's Pillow* website.

About the Author

Linda Silbert

Daughter of Ann Dreizen Bress and granddaughter of Bessie Markman Dreizen, Linda Silbert was born and raised in New Rochelle, New York. When she was 11 years old, her family moved a few miles north to Eastchester.

Linda and her husband Al, both of whom have doctorates in education, are the owners of Strong Learning, Inc., a well-known tutoring company in the New York area. They are the award-winning authors of a variety of educational books and games, including *Why Bad Grades Happen to Good Kids* and its soon-to-be-released companion book, *Why Bad Grades Happen to Good Teachers*.

Bessie's Pillow is Linda's first novel.

--◦═◉═◦--

For additional information about *Bessie's Pillow*
or to contact the author or publisher, please visit:
www.BessiesPillow.com

--◦═◉═◦--